iva frowned. 'What are you suggesting?'

'You both co...

'Live with y... ...on a squeak.

'*Si.*'

'As your kept woman?' Shrugging off his hands, she brought herself round to face him, leaning back on her elbows, her small breasts thrust tantalisingly upwards. 'What are you proposing, Damiano? A life of luxury for the little upstart…' she couldn't keep the hurt out of her voice '…in exchange for custody of Ben, with the odd sexual favour thrown in?'

His face was a chiselled rock against the hard blue of the sky. 'May I remind you that he's my son too?' He sounded quietly angry. 'And, no. *Santo cielo!* That isn't what I'm proposing.'

'What, then?'

'I think we should marry,' he said.

Elizabeth Power wanted to be a writer from a very early age, but it wasn't until she was nearly thirty that she took to writing seriously. Writing is now her life. Travelling ranks very highly among her pleasures, and so many places she has visited have been recreated in her books. Living in England's West Country, Elizabeth likes nothing better than taking walks with her husband along the coast or in the adjoining woods, and enjoying all the wonders that nature has to offer.

SINS OF THE PAST

BY
ELIZABETH POWER

First published in Great Britain 2011
by Mills & Boon, an imprint of Harlequin (UK) Limited,
Eton House, 18-24 Paradise Road, Richmond, Surrey TW9 1SR

© Elizabeth Power 2011

ISBN: 978 0 263 88658 0

Harlequin (UK) policy is to use papers that are natural, renewable and recyclable products and made from wood grown in sustainable forests. The logging and manufacturing process conform to the legal environmental regulations of the country of origin.

Printed and bound in Spain
by Blackprint CPI, Barcelona

SINS OF THE PAST

FOR ALAN—for everything

PROLOGUE

SANTO cielo! It was *her*!

With his skill at addressing the immediate, whilst keeping abreast of everything else going on around him, Damiano responded to something the woman behind the desk was saying, though his glittering black eyes were trained on the younger woman who had stopped briefly in the corridor beyond the glass partition.

Red hair—not long, as he remembered it, but short and fashionably tousled. She looked, with that natural curve to her mouth and those small pointed features, like some mischievous elf. Yet it was a mischief, he acknowledged through a rising tide of shock, motivated by opportunism and greed.

'Mr D'Amico?'

Immaculate dark tailoring couldn't hide the whipcord strength and physical power of a man in the peak of condition, a man of impressionable force and character, whose striking features were hardening now as he brought himself back sharply to the matter in hand.

How could he allow just one glimpse of that redhead to cause his concentration to slide? He had business to attend to. A chain of leisure centres and retail outlets to get up and running. But when he had arranged this meeting to finalise details with the design team who handled all his UK developments, he hadn't expected to come in and be confronted by a ghost from his past.

'That girl…' She hadn't seen him! He had only an impression now of feathery strands against an elegantly pale neck as she let herself into the office opposite the one in which he was standing and disappeared from view.

'You mean Miss Singleman?' His associate's eyes had followed his, her swept up black hair and dramatically red lips emphasising the hard edge of a successful businesswoman in her fifties. But she knew who had been stealing his attention. 'Riva?'

'Riva…' The word rolled off his tongue as sensually as it was savoured. So she was still unmarried. *'Sì.'* He was trying to appear calm. Calmer than he felt! he decided, annoyed. His manner, though, demanded more, and the woman smiled, supplying it.

'One of our newest recruits. She specialises in the domestic environment at present. She's young, enthusiastic, a bit off-beat sometimes in her approach, but very, very talented.'

As well as untrustworthy and a scheming liar!

For one fleeting moment he fought the urge to walk out and take his future business elsewhere, rather than let a company who could employ the type of questionable character it had obviously employed with Miss Riva Singleman loose with his money. But intrigue as to how such a dubious little drop-out could possibly have come to be working for such a reputable firm of interior designers, along with the memory of how that lying little mouth had felt beneath his, got the better of him. He had never been faint-hearted. So why shouldn't he get his business sorted out, accept the opportunity that fate had suddenly presented him with, and satisfy his curiosity along the way?

He listened to the matriarch of Redwood Interiors assuring him that everything was going to schedule, with all his wishes being met, and that whatever members of her team were allotted to handle his affairs at any time would give him no less than two hundred per cent satisfaction.

Like hell they would! he resolved, and gave the woman one

of his blazing smiles, charming her witless as he had been doing with women for the whole of his thirty-two years, as he settled on his suddenly innovative and calculating plan.

CHAPTER ONE

RIVA pulled up outside the stone building on the fringes of what had once been a thriving country estate. She could see the old manor house at the end of the long drive, boarded up, uninhabited. A *'For Sale'* sign hung haphazardly on one of its rusty gates.

But it was the building in front of her that drew her attention as she stepped out of her car onto the gravelled courtyard. *The Old Coach House.*

Once a stable-block for the manor, this place looked very much inhabited. A couple of other vehicles—one a gleaming black Porsche—were parked outside.

Her light mood was enhanced by the chirruping birds and the late spring sunlight filtering down through the trees as she locked her small hatchback and tripped eagerly across the gravel. Her first real big job where she was to be given carte blanche! To conceptualise and co-ordinate all the furnishings, colours and textures for a special room inside this wonderful old house. What an opportunity!

Her hand was trembling with excitement as she pressed the gleaming brass doorbell. Her portfolio had obviously impressed someone so much that they had asked for her specifically, and if she could pull off this job to everyone's satisfaction it could be the making of her career! No more struggling to make ends meet—to keep a very necessary roof over her head. And if she was valued enough to be given the chance to immerse herself in a project like this, perhaps one day her dreams of owning her own studio might turn into a reality, and all the anguish she'd endured over the past few years would be a thing of the past.

'Madame Duval?'

The chic blonde in the charcoal-grey suit who opened the door to her was assessing Riva's less conventional attire with a quizzical smile.

'No. *Madame*'s not here, but you are expected. Miss Singleman, isn't it?'

Riva nodded and followed in a slipstream of exotic perfume as she was guided up some stairs into the main body of the house. At only five feet three inches she felt dwarfed by the other girl's height, and wondered whether she should have worn high heels, or even a jacket, but she hated conformity. Until the other woman had opened the door she had felt smart in the belted black and grey striped tunic she had teamed with a short black skirt, dark leggings and pumps.

'If you'll just wait here...'

Riva glanced around on finding herself alone in a large, sunny sitting room overlooking the courtyard. Whoever had furnished this heart of the house had taste and style, she decided, if the faultless décor and exemplary furnishings were anything to go by. There was a mix of fine prints—an aerial shot of some tropical islands, some brightly coloured fish, and the most spectacular palm-fringed beach imaginable—adorning the walls.

'Well, well. If it isn't Miss Riva Singleman.'

The deeply-accented voice, dark as velvet, enlivened every nerve with its dangerous familiarity.

She swung round so fast that the bag dangling from her hand struck the leg of a small Georgian table, almost toppling the delicate but vastly expensive-looking vase that was standing on top.

'I do hope this isn't an indication that you're going to be accident-prone.'

Tall, olive-skinned, too strong-featured to be called con-ventionally handsome, the man in the dark suit standing in the doorway was everything she remembered: impeccably dressed, with sleek raven hair combed straight back. His face was a familiar maze of striking angles and exciting complex-ity, from his high forehead and sculpted cheekbones to the arrogant nose and the hard, wide mouth that was curling now in patent mockery of her clumsiness.

'*Damiano!*'

If he was surprised to see her, he wasn't showing it. Every inch of that lean and disciplined physique exuded command, self-confidence, poise, as did his easy stride as he came into the room, studying her with those penetrating dark eyes and those cunning wits that once had lured her into trusting him. Much to her cost, she reflected bitterly.

'I thought...' She was toying agitatedly with the black and grey beaded necklace which lay just above her small breasts. What was he doing here? From what she'd read about him nowadays his UK home was a bachelor apartment in the most fashionable suburb of London. Not this quiet, countrified retreat...

'You thought what?' He sent a cursory glance over his shoulder, following the direction of her gaze. 'My secretary,' he enlightened her, answering her unspoken question. 'She was simply handling the appointment.'

And probably a lot more than that, Riva thought waspishly, thinking of the string of stunning high-profile women she had seen his name linked with in the gossip columns over the years. She remembered one article in particular in one of the tabloids recently, featuring society queen and grocery empire heiress Magenta Boweringham, who, being the latest lover to be discarded by this dynamic Italian, had gone to great lengths to report that, however brilliant and focused he might have proved himself to be in every other aspect of his life, where her own sex were concerned, Damiano D'Amico seemed to have a very low boredom threshold.

Ignoring a resurgence of the feelings she had had after reading that article, Riva uttered, baffled, 'Madame Duval...' Her tousled red hair caught the morning sunlight streaming in through the long sash window as she shook her head, trying to make sense of the situation.

'My grandmother,' he supplied, his easy tone only emphasising her confusion. 'Obviously you weren't told she was away.'

'No, I wasn't!' Hot colour washed over her skin and she let her hand drop quickly when his gaze fell, picking up on the agitated way she was fingering her necklace. His grandmother was *French*? Her head was swimming. She wasn't sure he had ever told her that. 'Did you know?' she demanded. 'Did you know it was me Redwoods were sending?' Her name must have aroused his interest, if nothing else.

A wide shoulder merely lifted beneath the fine cloth of his jacket. 'It does leave me wondering how a girl who was little more than a market trader a few short years ago,' he said, not answering her, 'managed to reach the position she's obviously enjoying now.'

'She worked!' Rose colour deepened along her cheekbones, vying with the fire of her hair. 'She worked, Damiano! Which is more than she's going to do for you!'

Angrily she brushed past him, her suspicions and disappointment over not being engaged solely on her merits overridden only by her staggering awareness of his masculinity as her arm collided with his.

Shaking from the contact, in a voice that reflected all the tension that was gripping her, she uttered, 'I'll tell Ms Redwood that it's all been a mistake. Now, if you don't mind, I think I can manage to see myself out!'

Disillusionment contested with a host of other, more complex emotions as she made her determined bid for the stairs. Only the deep, accented voice behind her stopped her precipitate flight along the corridor.

'I really don't think you should do that, Riva.' Those dangerously soft words masked a barely concealed threat.

'Wh-what do you mean?' She turned around to see him dominating the narrow space outside the sitting room, and for all her twenty-four years she felt as out of her depth with him as she had as a hapless nineteen-year-old, smitten by that voice, by his earth-shattering looks, his intellect, and his irresistible Continental charm.

'You've been sent here for a specific purpose, and I expect you to honour that purpose. Otherwise I shall have no hesitation in telling your very hard-nosed employer that I shall be taking my business elsewhere.'

A car engine starting up in the courtyard below the window broke the small shocked silence that stretched between them.

His secretary leaving. Leaving her alone with him, Riva decided, with an inexplicable little shudder.

Her blood started pounding, a thundering drum-roll in her ears. Of course. He was more valuable to Redwoods than she was, she realised. And if she refused to work with him, and he reported her lack of co-operation, then it would be her the firm would let go for losing such a prestigious client—not the other way around.

The green eyes looking up into the dark ebony of his sparked with accusation. 'You mean…you'd get me fired?' Her voice was strung with anger, disbelief.

His shoulder moved again in that subtly careless gesture. 'You'd get yourself fired, Riva. Or not. The choice is yours.'

And if she made the wrong one, refused to do exactly as he said, he would destroy her. Just as he had destroyed her dear and oh, so vulnerable mother, because without his cruel intervention Chelsea Singleman would almost surely be alive today!

'Go back into the sitting room,' he ordered, in no doubt of the power he wielded.

Reminding herself of how hard she'd worked for this job,

and of all she had to lose if she walked away from him, Riva thrust past him again, steeling herself against the sensations that assailed her this time when he didn't move to allow her an easy route back and once again her arm grazed the sleeve of his jacket.

'Do that again and I'll take it that you're inviting more than just my custom. And we both know what happened the last time you did that, don't we?'

He had used her, ruthlessly and cold-bloodedly, employing that lethal mix of easy charm and magnetism to snare her. She had been too naïve and inexperienced to recognise the calculated game he was playing, only realising it afterwards with her pride and her dignity in shreds!

'I didn't invite your custom, Damiano. You're forcing it on me.'

'Like you've probably convinced yourself it was me forcing you…what was it?…four and a half—nearly five years ago?'

Surprisingly, the vital images his words conjured up still had the power to make her blood race, the memory of those warm, skilled hands on her body making her cheeks flame with humiliating shame.

Because she had been a willing conquest beneath those practised hands of his, mindlessly inviting their intimate caresses, mistaking tenderness for affection, his cold, calculated seduction for something much, much more.

Acridly she murmured, 'No. That was nothing more than my own stupidity.'

That dark head tilted slightly, and a humourless smile still played around the corners of his devastating mouth.

'You could scarcely blame me for wanting to get at the truth.'

'The truth? Hah! You wouldn't recognise the truth if it uprooted itself and tried to wrap itself around your throat!'

He smiled coldly at her graphic metaphor. 'I didn't have to. All the evidence spoke for itself.'

Because she had lied to him—and big-time!—covering up even the most personal facts about herself. But only because she had been embarrassed, so unbearably ashamed. He'd been angry with her afterwards, but more, she'd suspected, with himself. Perhaps finding out he'd used a virgin in his plan to destroy Chelsea Singleman didn't sit too comfortably on his conscience. If he had one! Riva thought vehemently, although she doubted it.

Green eyes glittering with a host of complex emotions, she breathed accusingly, 'You ruined my mother's life.'

Damiano's mouth moved grimly. 'Because I was instrumental in preventing her from marrying my uncle? I would have been guilty of neglecting my duty if I hadn't. Anyway, I'm sure she got over it. Women like Chelsea—and I'm afraid to say like you, *cara*—aren't left grieving too long over one lost opportunity. If she hasn't done so yet, I'm sure that before long she'll find some other rich…what do you English call it?…*sucker* who will fall prey to her devious charms.'

Pain as sharp as a whiplash cut into Riva's heart, and it took all her self-control to stop herself lunging forward and knocking the disdain right off that hard, arrogant face.

'My mother's dead!'

His obvious shock was a picture she would have relished if she hadn't felt so raw inside.

The sound of a man whistling for his dog in the quiet lane beyond the courtyard filtered through the open window—the only thing intruding on the loaded silence.

'I'm sorry.'

She'd have to admit that he looked it, if she hadn't known him to be incapable of such selfless emotion.

'No, you're not.' How could he even say that when he had contributed so directly to the woman's inevitable slide into the despair that had finally killed her—and at such a brutally young age?

'What happened?'

'What do you care?'

His features hardened at her lack of response. 'Tell me.'

She didn't want to. It hurt too much to talk about her once effervescent young mother—who had insisted on Riva calling her Chelsea—especially in front of the one man she had hoped never to see again.

His whole demeanour, however, commanded, and reluctantly she found herself yielding to the sway of his forceful personality by saying, 'If you must know, it was an accidental overdose of drugs she'd been taking for depression.' She had also been drinking too, although she didn't tell him that. The doctors had said it was a lethal mix.

'When?'

'Just over a year ago.'

That firm mouth compressed. 'As I said, I'm sorry.'

She gave a brittle little laugh. 'Don't be. After all, it wasn't *your* fault she sank into depression after her wrecked engagement to the man she loved!'

'You're holding me responsible for that?'

'If the cap fits.'

'Unfortunately, Riva, it doesn't.' He glanced across to the window, his clean-shaven yet darkly shadowed jaw a statement to his hard and potent virility. 'You know full well why Marcello broke off his engagement to your mother,' he stated with dogmatic cruelty. 'She was investigated and found wanting. You both were.'

'Yes, but only by you!'

'Because Marcello was too bewitched by a pretty face and a pair of dancing blue eyes to see beyond the superficially sweet smiles and the cleverly crafted cover-up.'

'Which you weren't, of course?'

'Hardly.' His jaw-line hardened as he expounded. 'And, while my uncle might have been treated to a watered-down version of the truth from your mother, he wasn't the one chosen to be the recipient of the most blatant lies.'

He was talking about her, and she cringed now at the elaborate story she had woven around herself, around her background and her upbringing, shuddering from her naïveté in believing he would never find out. Nothing, though, could reverse that, and she could never tell him exactly why she had lied.

'Now, if it's all the same to you, you won't mind if we get on and do the job you've been sent here to do.' His outstretched arm demanded that she precede him out of the room.

Glad to let their conversation drop, Riva complied.

Watching the way she moved as he directed her back downstairs to the room he wanted redesigning, he couldn't help noticing the proud little tilt to her pointed chin and the slim back held straight as a rod beneath the soft jersey top.

She had spirit. He had to hand her that.

He caught a waft of her perfume, flowery and fresh, and felt a kick in his loins that shook him to the very core of his being.

With that fiery hair, that milky skin, and breasts that certainly couldn't be called buxom, she wasn't the tall, blonde, leggy type he usually gravitated towards, but there was something about her…something that attracted him even as it irritated him. He was having to acknowledge that he still wanted the arty little creature, as he had wanted her from the moment he had first laid eyes on her all those years ago in his uncle's villa.

When Marcello had informed him that he was getting married, he'd been naturally delighted, he remembered. His uncle—his late father's brother—had been a widower for more than ten years. But Damiano couldn't deny that when he had arrived at the villa at Marcello's invitation, to meet his proposed new bride, he had been shocked to discover a woman half Marcello's age with a fully-grown daughter in tow.

At first he had thought they were sisters. On first name terms, and so alike in build and stature, with their loose floral skirts and their long straight hair—except that, unlike the vibrant redhead, the other had been a platinum blonde.

· He had been dubious about them from the start. Who were they? Where had they come from, with their joss-sticks and their beads and their home-made sandals, which the younger of the two had often preferred to discard? And what woman, still only in her thirties—as he'd discovered the older one was—would want to tie herself to a handsome, yet nevertheless elderly widower? Unless she was attracted less to his warmth and generosity of spirit than to his status as head of one of the oldest families in Italy, with all the money and influence that went with it?

That Marcello had plucked them both from a market stall selling hand-made jewellery in some English seaside resort had only fuelled Damiano's need to find out more about them, since his uncle had been too infatuated with his new fiancée even to want to know or care.

He had put his own staff on the job, and set about pumping the more reserved though equally—as he'd believed—worldly daughter for all the information he could get out of her, while maintaining his resolve not to let her get to him in any way.

Her father, she'd told him, had been an officer in the Royal Navy. A brave man, decorated for services to his country, who'd been away from home a lot while she had been growing up. Chelsea, she had convinced him, could have used her talents as a commercial artist, but her husband had always frowned on her having her own career, believing that it was demeaning for the wife of a man in his position to have to work. He had given Riva the best possible education, she had told him with undisguised admiration, but then he'd been tragically killed in a car crash while on leave. He had left her and her mother well provided for, she had gone on to assure him, although the lovely house where they'd lived had been far too big for the two of them after he'd died.

She had given him more—far more—than he could ever have expected, he thought grimly, and not just information.

A nerve twitched in his jaw as he thought about it, because even now it still rankled with him that he had deflowered a virgin in his determination to get at the truth. Yet he had salved his conscience by assuring himself that in going to bed with him the scheming little witch must have had a very marked agenda of her own.

He shuddered now as he thought of the consequences that falling for her charade of experience and sophistication could have brought down on his head, because he had been proved right by the team he had paid to check out both her and her mother.

They were drop-outs, protest marchers—troublemakers, in his opinion—and, as he'd suspected all along, just a pair of gold-diggers. Nothing Riva had told him had held a gram of truth.

Born illegitimate to parents who had never bothered to marry, she had come from a grossly under-privileged area, attending only basic, run-of the-mill state schools. Her mother, far from being a potential career woman, had found it hard holding down even the most menial job to pay the rent—or not, as the fancy took her—on a changing assortment of cheap, downmarket digs. The closest her father had come to being a 'naval man'—as both Chelsea and Riva had referred to him— was when he'd been employed for a time unloading barges, and the only uniform he had worn had been inside one of Her Majesty's prisons, where he'd been serving a well-earned sentence for fraud! The one scrap of authenticity in the whole story was that he *had* been killed in a car accident—the year after his release and under the influence of drink!

That he had saved his uncle from the clutches of such a dubious pair of women was something Damiano would continue to be thankful for. He regretted what had happened to Chelsea Singleman. *Per amor di Dio!* He would hardly be human if he didn't! But it was galling to realise that if she had married his uncle, who had sadly died after a short illness eighteen months ago, and Marcello had left everything to his grieving widow, then because of Chelsea's unfortunate death since, this little opportunist would now be enjoying the benefits of all Marcello D'Amico's wealth!

'So what do you think?' His voice was harsh from the turn his thoughts had taken as he watched her surveying what the studio had informed her was to be redesigned as a crafts and hobbies room. 'We were imagining something with more of a Continental feel, perhaps. Are you up to the task?'

Riva took in the rather drab décor and the few pieces of furniture—mostly covered in dust sheets, apart from a tall bookcase and a large rectangular table that stood against one wall. It was a room obviously designed as a private sanctuary, tucked away at the back of the house. She could see that someone—perhaps the woman herself—had already tried to add a classical feel and fallen far short of what they had been intending. The only redeeming feature was the pair of floor-to-ceiling doors that looked out onto a quiet terrace—although some of the paving stones were broken. There was a pleasing aspect of the old manor, though, she noted, through the specimen trees.

Meeting that hostile masculine gaze now, she said, 'Are you asking me—or telling me?'

'I take it it's within your capabilities?' he pursued, ignoring her barbed question, and didn't fail to notice the way her tight little mouth compressed.

He had her where he wanted her—jumping to his command—and she knew it, he realised. He derived a rather guilty pleasure from that.

'What does your grandmother do?' Grudgingly she moved away into the centre of the room, studying its lay-out, its dimensions, its position—whether or not it faced the sun. There was nothing, though, not even in the empty bookcases, she realised, dropping her bag down on the table, to give her any clue as to the woman's character.

'Do?'

'Yes.' She swung round to see him frowning. 'Her crafts and hobbies? What are they?'

He gave a barely discernible shrug. 'She reads. She stitches. She...er...*ricamare*...'

'Embroiders?' Riva supplied, guessing that that was the word that was eluding him. 'So...she sews.' With a little inward smile she turned away from his disturbing scrutiny and that powerful aura of sexuality he exuded, which even now—even after what he had done—turned her knees to jelly, making her breathless, her pulse throb a little too hard.

'This room faces north, so the light stays constant... Perhaps one wall with a hint of colour...' She was already planning, feeling her enthusiasm building—despite everything; getting excited. It always happened when she was handed a project. Even now, when the dealer of that project was the man she despised more than anyone else in the world. But it was her job, and she was a professional. She didn't intend letting old hostilities stand in the way of her career. 'If we enlarge on the classical theme...' She was thinking aloud. 'Does she like Grecian?'

'Definitely.'

She glanced at him, wondering why he sounded so un-interested. Perhaps he thought his grandmother's need for a sewing room trivial and frivolous, she considered waspishly, deciding that she would do her best to please the old lady, even if it bored the socks off her superior grandson!

'Those patio doors supply adequate light...but it still needs brightening up.' She was assessing the space behind her. 'It's long enough and wide enough. Perhaps something on that wall...something bold and dramatic...' She was getting carried away, but stopped suddenly, her arm suspended in mid-air. 'Do you find something amusing?' she challenged pointedly.

Arms folded, leaning back against the bookcase, the man

was watching her with mocking insolence. 'On the contrary.' His mouth pulled down at one side. 'I'm rather impressed.'

'What did you expect?' she retorted, in no mood to be gracious. 'That I'd be out of my depth?'

'Like you were before?' Letting his arms fall, he moved away from the bookcase, a figure of such predatory watchfulness and cool intimidation that Riva brought her tongue nervously across her top lip.

Refusing, though, to be drawn into any further discussion with him on that subject, or anything else but the reason why she was there, she said pithily, 'That was then, Damiano—this is now. And if you don't mind I'd like to get on with the job the studio are paying me to do!'

She pivoted away from him, but, her temper still roused, she turned back and flung at him, 'Why me? In view of what you think you know about me, aren't you worried that I might decide the job isn't really worth all the hassle? That I might decide it would simply benefit me more just to take off with a few of your—of your grandmother's—priceless antiques?'

His mouth twisted speculatively as he weighed up that last comment.

'One.' He started counting out points. "Regardless of what you say to the contrary, I'm sure you value your job far too much. Two. There isn't anything in this house worth more than having my curiosity satisfied. And three...' His voice had grown dangerously soft. 'Don't fool yourself into thinking you'd find me a very lenient master if I had to come after you, Riva. You seem to be forgetting that I've dealt with you before, and I'd certainly have no qualms about dealing with you again.'

She wasn't sure what he meant by *dealing with her*, but she certainly wasn't going to take a chance on finding out. He was a ruthless adversary—as she knew all too well from the unscrupulous methods he had used to bring her to her knees before.

Her cheeks burned from the memory as she fought a whole heap of repressed anger and frustration.

Damiano. She'd looked it up once. The definition had said *'one who subdues and tames'.*

Well, you won't tame me, Mr High-and-Mighty D'Amico! her brain screamed silently. But from the smile that played around his lips she knew that her body language alone had conveyed the rebellion in her.

'You asked why you?' Slipping a hand into the pocket of superbly tailored trousers, he perched on the edge of the table, one long leg at full stretch, the other hanging free. 'Apart from the obvious, when my secretary rang the studio to book a consultant she was offered a very glowing report on your capabilities. In fact she was supplied with some very interesting facts about you.'

No, please!

Her heart had started racing and her stomach muscles clenched almost sickeningly. What had the studio let slip?

She saw the furrow pleating the tanned masculine forehead and wondered if the overriding feeling of panic she was experiencing was stamped all over her face.

'I understand you've been there less than a year. You did a design course at home, and have more talent and flair with your limited experience than all the team at Redwoods had had at your level put together.'

Letting her breath out very slowly, Riva prompted, 'Anything else?' She felt—and sounded even to her own ears—as though she'd been running hard.

'Well, that you excelled at art—' his smile was feral '—but then I knew that already, didn't I?'

Because they had talked for all those weeks when she'd felt herself blossoming in his company, opening up to him, imagining that she could trust him. While all the time she had been unintentionally helping to condemn herself in his eyes—along with her mother.

'Anything else?' Fear and her hatred of him laced her voice with sarcasm. 'Like my favourite colour? What DVDs I watch? My favoured breakfast cereal?'

'None of those things,' he assured her with mocking amusement. 'Particularly the breakfast menu. But as we're to be working together perhaps we can reacquaint ourselves with the…finer facets of each other's natures over the next few weeks.'

His scarcely veiled meaning made her tense. He might have other ideas, but there was no way, she assured herself, she would be allowing him into her private life.

'Don't hold your breath on that, Damiano. As far as I'm concerned you're the lowest of the low. You might not be giving me any choice about working for you, but I do still have some say over the company I keep outside of working hours—and as far as including you in that company is concerned, I'd rather shack up with a rat!'

'A very interesting notion.' Surprisingly, he was still looking amused—as though her heated outburst had left him totally unmoved. 'Well, as I said…' He stood up now, the power and grace of his body causing Riva's throat to go dry as the smile slid from his face, assuring her of how dangerous it would be ever to underestimate him, as he advised. 'Shall we get on?'

And that was it? No more questions? No more startling revelations that the studio had carelessly disclosed about her?

'That's why I'm here.' Her own imitation of a smile felt painfully stretched.

He didn't know! Why should he? she reasoned hectically, her shoulders slumping with a relief that left her weak. All she had to do now was offer her advice and her skills in the way she was being paid to do, get the job done, and get out. The fact that the frighteningly potent sexuality she'd been powerless to resist before seemed to have strengthened a thousandfold since she had seen him last was something she was going to have to put up with. She only knew she would have to guard herself against it—against him—and not let her defences down for a second. After all, she wasn't the infatuated nineteen-year-old who had fallen for him hook, line and sinker. She was a woman now, with a home and a career and the sense and wisdom to resist men like Damiano D'Amico.

The only thing that mattered was that by some miracle he didn't know the most important thing about her, and she was going to do everything in her power to make sure that he never did.

CHAPTER TWO

'WHO's a lucky girl, then? Working for Damiano D'Amico?' one of Redwood's more experienced female designers declared enviously to Riva, who had just rushed into the office,

'What?' Flushed, feeling as though she'd been juggling twenty balls in the air to get to the studio this morning, Riva frowned. How could anyone else have known when she hadn't even known herself until yesterday?

'What's she got that the rest of us haven't got?' another woman asked, a little less warmly.

'Mystery, darling,' one of the young men from Graphics piped up as he was passing. 'Men are fascinated by enigmas—especially ones that come in small and interesting packages. She also brings out their protective streak—unlike the rest of you amazons.'

Riva shot a friendly reprimand at him, leaving a series of guffaws behind her as she made her way to her boss's office. It didn't matter how big or how small you were, she thought poignantly. A man like Damiano could still rip the heart out of you—with no trouble at all.

'So how did it go yesterday?'

Brisk, forceful and efficient, her make-up as striking as ever, Olivia Redwood was leaning across her desk, eager for a report on the previous day's assignment.

'I didn't realise that this Madame Duval was a relation of Damiano D'Amico's,' Riva stated cagily.

'No, I didn't make the connection myself until he rang yesterday afternoon to confirm that you'd do nicely. But apparently it was Damiano who specifically requested you in the first place, Riva—not his grandmother, as I previously thought. I did think he seemed rather taken with you when he came in to see us last week.'

'He *what*?'

'Yes, you should consider yourself honoured,' the woman went on, oblivious to how shaken Riva was. 'Isn't he a personable character?' Even the no-nonsense queen of Redwood Interiors couldn't conceal her appreciation of the impressive Mr Damiano D'Amico. 'And so handsome—in a forceful sort of way!'

Beneath the dark blue silk top worn over fitted black trousers Riva shrugged, quietly seething. 'And disgustingly rich too. A definite advantage for anyone on the receiving end of his business,' she added, with more venom than she knew was wise.

'You don't sound particularly enamoured.' Shrewd dark eyes were studying her dubiously. 'There isn't one woman in this company who wouldn't give her right arm to be given the opportunity to work for the family—let alone be especially chosen by Damiano himself.'

Riva shrugged again, trying to make light of it. 'I'm afraid my arms are pretty much needed where they are.'

Olivia's smile was fleeting. She wasn't prone to discussing domestic issues in the office. 'Now, you do appreciate that Mr D'Amico is one of our most valued clients—so no outspokenness.'

Because she was renowned for it, Riva realised with a mental grimace. 'Of course.'

'I've heard he can be a hard taskmaster, as well as a consummate perfectionist, but then he wouldn't be the success story he obviously is if he didn't run a tight ship and expect anyone who works for him to tow the line. We're only as good as the last job we do for him, so this company's relying on you to ensure we continue to secure all his return custom. Bear that in mind.'

'Of course,' Riva reiterated, wondering what the woman would say if she knew the things her newest employee had flung at her most treasured client the previous day. Olivia was generous towards her staff, and had given Riva's career a kick-start in the world of interior design because she had seen her potential. Even so, Olivia Redwood was a canny businesswoman, and Riva knew there would be no tolerance or favouritism if she did anything to jeopardise the firm's success.

'He seemed to know a lot about me.' Reaching the door, Riva turned back, her fingers unusually tense around the door handle.

'He's a very important man. He naturally wanted some insight into how long you had been here and how qualified you were before taking you on.'

'But you didn't tell him about…my situation?' she ventured hesitantly.

'Was I supposed to?' Riva looked quickly away from the speculative eyes. 'I didn't think he'd want to know about your private life, Riva. You can tell him yourself if—or when—the need arises. Apart from which, I didn't want to say anything that might deter him from engaging you. I'm giving you a chance, Riva. Don't blow it. We've got targets to reach, and I'm counting on you to make sure we reach them.'

She spent the rest of the morning working on paperwork for a job she was winding up. Then after lunch, armed with her laptop and her camera, she set off to take photographs of the room she was redesigning at the Old Coach House, as arranged with Damiano the previous day.

Letting herself in with the key he had given her, though he had said he would be back there again today, all her tensions released themselves with bone-weakening relief when she discovered that the place was empty—which left her free to get on with her planning without the distraction of the man's disturbing presence.

It was much later in the afternoon when she heard a car growl into the cobbled courtyard at the front of the house, and instantly her whole body tightened up.

The desire to trip along the hall and sneak a glimpse out of the window was curbed by the mortifying thought of Damiano seeing her—because there was no doubt, from the throbbing power of that engine, that it was him.

Every tight, tense cell alerted Riva to the front door closing a few moments later, and then that steady stride coming along the hall, and her fingers were making nonsense of the characters on her computer screen as she tried to keep typing, feigning a total lack of interest in his arrival.

'*Buon giorno.*' The velvety softness of his greeting made her look up, and she wished she hadn't when the sheer impact of his masculinity made her tongue cleave to the roof of her mouth.

Sleek black hair—damp, as if he had just showered—accentuated the pristine whiteness of his shirt, which was partially unbuttoned, exposing the crisp dark hair of his olive-skinned chest. His arm was resting against the doorjamb, and where the jacket of his light beige suit had parted she could see how tight and firm his waistline was, how the fabric of his trousers stretched across the hard, lean breadth of his hips.

'Were you so engrossed in your innovative ideas that you didn't hear me come in, Riva? Or is it a determined effort on your part to show me that you aren't the least bit interested one way or the other?'

She shivered at how easily he could read her.

'You lied to me,' she breathed accusingly. She didn't have to enlighten him. He knew exactly what she was talking about.

'That makes two of us.' There wasn't an ounce of compunction in that lean, hard body as he strode in.

She glanced quickly away as he came towards her, uncertain

which part of his splendid anatomy she'd feel comfortable looking at. What chance had she had against that potent masculinity, she thought, when she had been a naïve creature of nineteen?

'I was beginning to think you wouldn't be here today.' That was preferable to asking him why he'd lied. She knew why. He'd known she would have wriggled out of the job if she'd been forewarned.

'I forgot to mention that I was scheduled for a couple of very punishing hours of squash this afternoon.'

'Really?' She didn't believe that a man as influential and powerful as Damiano D'Amico would forget anything. He had probably relished the thought of keeping her in suspense as to when he was coming back! 'Did you win?' She didn't know why she asked it. She couldn't imagine anyone punishing him—in any sense whatsoever. Physically he was built like a god who paid homage to health and strength and fitness, and heaven help anyone who tried to pit their wits against that awesome brain!

'It was a satisfactory outcome.'

'Satisfactory for you? Or for your opponent?' She didn't need to ask. She just couldn't seem to contain the desire to bait him at every given opportunity. And that way lay disaster if she had any intention of hanging on to her job, she reminded herself sharply.

The freshness of the shower gel that still clung to his body invaded her nostrils as he came over to the table where she was sitting and picked up a sheet of paper, examining the various sketches that she had been making.

'I would have thought experience would have taught you, Riva. I always play to win.'

She sucked in an audible breath. 'No matter who gets hurt?' She couldn't look at him as she said it. She couldn't seem to breathe either, too aware of his scent, the sound of his voice, his disconcerting nearness, and, as he returned her sketches to the table, of the dark lean strength of his hands.

'No one gets hurt as long as they know their limits,' he assured her, 'and don't indulge in games which are totally out of their league. But if you're referring to that little game you were playing with me in the past—which I'm sure you are—don't try and pretend to me that I hurt you, Riva. Oh, perhaps a little physically—but then you didn't exactly prepare me for your...innocence.' His voice derided. As well it might, she realised bitterly. A virgin she might have been, but he hadn't seen her sacrifice and everything that had led up to it as anything other than part of a calculated plan. 'If you had, I would never have let things get so out of hand.'

'What would you have done?' Her tone was wounded, hurt, shrill. 'Locked me in a room and used an interrogation lamp on me instead? Well, if it's any consolation to your macho pride and your failing judgement about me, I would never have gone to bed with you if I'd known I'd be sleeping with a snake!'

'What did you expect? That I'd be taken in as easily as Marcello? The fact is it is something that we both have to live with. But just for the record...I don't recall that much sleeping was done.'

Wings of bright colour suffused her pale cheeks, and she felt decidedly sticky under her silky top.

Pushing herself disconcertedly to her feet, she crossed the room to put some distance between them, and started making more than a show of measuring the floor area. The red glow of the laser tape measure cut through the space like his brutality had once cut into her young, unsuspecting pride.

'As far as I'm concerned, Damiano, you were just an unfortunate episode in my life.'

'And how many more...fortunate episodes have there been, Riva?'

'That's none of your damn business!'

'Or should I amend that to profitable?'

'How dare you? You make me sound like...'

'Like what?'

Features contorted with disgust, she couldn't bring herself to answer. What was he saying? Who did he think he was?

'As you said to me… What was the expression again…? If the cap fits…'

'And as *you* said to me—' she was striding purposefully back across the room '—it doesn't!'

He was perched on the edge of the table as she came around the other side, putting the safe shield of her chair between them. She made a show of picking up papers, tidying them up and putting them down again. She wanted to sit down, get on with her work. She wished he would move.

'All right. So it's an episode we both want to forget. We both had an agenda. You lost. That's life. But, regardless of our individual motives, I don't think that either of us can deny that it was a very pleasurable experience.'

A small strangled sound escaped Riva, and the eyes she fixed on his were wide with disbelief. 'You're not for real! If you think I enjoyed it, then your ego's even bigger than I imagined it was. If you want the truth, the whole experience just made me sick!'

She wanted her stapler, which was on the other side of the table. She had to go around him to retrieve it and did so, giving him a significantly wide berth.

'I'm not a tyrant, *cara*, but if you're determined to treat me like one then we are not going to have a very satisfactory working relationship. And that's something I think we'd better put an end to right now.'

For a brief heart-sinking moment she thought that he was going to call it a day. Report back to the studio that she wasn't up to the job and get someone else to come in and work on his precious brief. Bitter experience, though, should have warned her about underestimating Damiano D'Amico: men like him didn't need anyone else to do their dirty work for them.

Perched, as he still was, on the edge of the table, when she made to move past him he reached out and in one fluid movement caught her by the wrist.

Her senses leaping, she felt the little blue vein beneath his thumb start to thrum with the blood that was pumping through her, and with sinking dismay knew that he could feel it too.

'I'm not afraid of you,' she murmured, the way her breath shivered through her from this devastating contact with him giving the lie to her trembling statement.

He smiled without warmth. 'Good.' His eyes were glittering like midnight pools in moonlight, so mesmerising that as he pulled her towards him she felt like a heap of pulsing jelly and could only clutch at the fabric of his other sleeve to stave off the feeling of tumbling down and down into their dangerous depths.

In a voice that was shaking as much as she was, she challenged, 'What do you think you're doing?'

His lips moved in a parody of a smile. 'I always believe in putting my theories into practice,' he said, his long ebony lashes coming down as those disturbing eyes dropped to the fullness of her trembling mouth, and before she could find her voice to demand what those theories were his face went out of focus and that mocking mouth was suddenly claiming hers.

He was still leaning against the table and, caught between his legs, she felt her senses start to reel from the warmth of his powerful thighs, from the movement of muscle beneath the quality cloth of his jacket, and from the hard insistence of his deepening kiss.

She had to stop this! Some smothered sense of reason tried to warn her that all he was doing was trying to humiliate her, make her pay for what she had just said to him, trying to cut her down to size.

As his arms tightened around her, though, her body paid no heed to the warning, letting her down as every galvanised cell leaped in recognition of his masculinity.

Her mouth widening beneath his, she gave a defeated little sound, the hands that had come up to grasp his shoulders now moving of their own volition to plunder the dark, damp hair at the nape of his neck.

Pulled closer against his hard, lean length, Riva gasped from the magnitude of her crazy response to him, sensations multiplying like locusts at the irrational thrill of this man's lips and hands that had once turned her into a woman with their skill and their expertise, this man who had been her first lover—and her last!

Rigid with a sexual tension she couldn't believe she was feeling, she heard a small voice inside her surface, to remind her of just how and why he had scarred her for any other man with his mind-blowing seduction before the cruel and devastating realisation that he had only been using her.

With a bitter little sob she wrenched herself away from him, and through gritted teeth managed to grind out, 'You conceited oaf!'

Though he had allowed her some merciful space, his hands were still gripping her shoulders. 'Deny it all you like,' he said, his strong features flushed, his breathing laboured. 'But we both know that your body is in conflict with that scheming little brain of yours, don't we? I might have exposed you and your mother for what you were, but there's much more to your venomous feeling for me than that, isn't there, Riva? You don't like me, *cara*, because of how I made you feel, because I reduced you to a whimpering mass of sensuality just begging me to take her, which didn't quite fit in with your plans to bring *me* to my knees and have me as putty in your greedy little hands.'

Which was what he had to keep reminding himself of, Damiano thought savagely, thrusting her away from him because—*mamma mia!*—it had only taken one kiss to convince him of how much he still wanted her. Even now the ache in his loins was so acute that it hurt.

'Believe that if you want to,' Riva retorted in a small, shaky voice, all the fight gone out of her after the shocking way she had responded to him—a man she hated, and with just cause!

Trembling from her response, and unsteadied by the way he had so brutally released her, she clutched at the table behind her, breathing deeply to try and regain some composure, staring at the broad span of his impeccably clad back.

It was no good reminding him of how his interference in her mother's affairs had indirectly caused the woman's death. She didn't even dare to goad him with that now.

He was angry—really angry—but there was something else, Riva realised. Something that had made him swing away from her, as though he couldn't bear to look at her. As though he were weary of the constant battle he was fighting with her. Or was it some sort of battle with himself?

Pulling herself up to her full height, which didn't seem to make a scrap of difference against his dominating six feet plus, surprisingly she found herself saying, 'If you've finished humiliating me, I've mapped out a few ideas on the computer that you might like to see.'

He was shrugging out of his jacket, tossing it down on a chair, and Riva averted her eyes from his hard, tanned torso—visible through the fine shirt—as he came and stooped over the table, pressing keys on her laptop, using the mouse himself.

'Olivia was right,' he said, after studying her ideas for a few breath-catching moments—because he was much too close, the sight and scent and sound of him invading her senses, and because she wanted his approval of her professional capabilities even if he despised every last bone in her body. 'You're very good.'

Such praise from him in the past would have made her glow with pleasure. All she felt now, though, was relieved acceptance and a strange, inexplicable regret.

'I like to think I'm a better judge of shapes and designs than I am of people,' she stated pointedly, glancing surreptitiously at her wristwatch when she thought he wasn't looking.

'Are you in some particular hurry to leave?' He was using

the scroll wheel, and hadn't even looked up from the screen. But then that shrewd brain of his wouldn't miss a thing, Riva decided, resenting him, resenting his cleverness, his sharp wits, his cold and calculating mind.

Nervously, she swallowed. 'I have an appointment.'

'An appointment?' He glanced up at her now, his dark eyes raking over her face. 'An appointment?' he repeated, straightening up. 'Or a hot date?'

She wouldn't tell him that she didn't date—not seriously, anyhow—any more than she would tell him that she'd been burned so badly by him during that summer in Italy that she had never allowed herself to get that close to any man since. But if he wanted to think that there was some man in her life who might mean something to her, then let him think it! she thought acridly. Perhaps that way, at least, she would be safe from him—and from herself!

'Damiano…' The sudden notion that she might need any protection from herself where he was concerned was as abominable as it was startling. Had she *wanted* him to kiss her? Surely not! Because if that was the case then she was no better than a Judas, even entertaining such ideas about him. How could she dismiss the way her mother had suffered— and at his hands? Forget her lack of will? The drinking? Her depressions?

He hadn't even responded to that last supplication. He was still contemplating the rough paper sketches she had made, no doubt mentally adding ideas of his own.

'Damiano…' It came out sounding much more desperate now. It was absolutely vital that she got away on time.

Casually he reached around her to drop the sketches down on the table, so close that the tangible warmth of his body made her drag in her breath.

'Who is this special person who makes you plead?' That familiar mocking smile was back, but there was curiosity too in those interrogative eyes.

'I'm not pleading.' Damn! Was that what he thought he could do to her? 'I just have to get away on time.'

He leaned back against the table and folded his arms, giving her all his attention now.

'This is no appointment, I think. Definitely a special date. Well, don't worry, *cara mia*. If he's worth his salt, he'll wait.'

Trying not to appear too alarmed, Riva shook her head. So much for letting him think there was another man in her life! 'I made a promise. I have to keep it.'

He picked up her mobile phone, which was lying close by. 'Then call him,' he invited, holding it out to her.

Trying to keep her anxiety in check, Riva snatched it from him. 'I don't need to,' she uttered, hating him provoking her like this. 'I just need to be on time!'

'So much devotion!' He was like a cat playing with a mouse, relishing every second of her discomfiture. 'He must be pretty special.'

Angrily, she snapped, 'He is!' then wished she hadn't, when those luxurious brown eyes narrowed to speculative slits and that hardening male mouth seemed to turn to stone.

'Does he know that another man only has to touch you to make you forget just how *special* he is.' His tone derided, and his cruel reminder of what had transpired a few moments ago made Riva's pale cheeks flame.

'If you're talking about your assault on me just now, I was taken totally off-guard, that was all.'

'Really?' Mockery gave a cruel curve to his lips again. 'In that case I'd be interested to witness how you'd react if I... *prepared* you, *carissima.*'

The deliberate hesitation, plus the endearment, were heavy with meaning, and she was reminded—as he'd intended her to be—of just how expertly he had 'prepared' her before.

That riveting sexual tension made her too slow to respond, and she stiffened as he spoke again in a voice now stripped of anything but professionalism.

'Is this what I am to expect? Your darting off at a moment's notice every time we have a meeting?'

'Of course not,' she uttered defensively, breathing again. 'It wouldn't have seemed like a moment's notice if you'd been here so I could let you know earlier that I had to get away sharply tonight.'

'Very well,' he conceded at last. 'As long as you realise in future that while you're doing this job your first loyalty is to me.'

Like hell! Riva thought, closing down her laptop before grabbing her bag and her papers and racing away.

CHAPTER THREE

THE clock on her dashboard was showing ten past five as she swung out of the cobbled courtyard and along the leafy lane towards the dual carriageway.

'How could it have happened?' she demanded fiercely of anyone who might be listening. How could she—after not seeing the detestable Damiano D'Amico for nearly five years—suddenly be working for him? And not just working for him—at his beck and call!

The snarl of her car's engine reflected her mood as she pulled out into the rush-hour traffic, and despite all the concentration needed to keep her mind on the road the past suddenly rushed upon her like a submerging tide.

Born when her mother was barely eighteen, Riva knew everything about deprivation and financial hardship. Her father she could only remember as a shadowy figure, flitting in and out of their lives, absent more than he was around. By the time she was old enough to know him he was already in prison, and that, and then his early death shortly afterwards, had plunged Riva and her mother into inescapable poverty.

Young, artistic and pretty, Chelsea had had no end of possible suitors who might have taken her and her daughter on. Strong-willed and free-spirited, though—a champion of causes—Chelsea Singleman had been determined to 'go it alone'.

Scarred and disillusioned after her experience with

Riva's father, her mother had always warned her of the dangers in succumbing to sexual desire. When Riva had met Damiano D'Amico, therefore, she had been ill-equipped to match his hard sophistication—which was why it had been so easy for him to turn her lack of experience to his own ends, she thought, hating him with a passion she couldn't believe she could feel for anyone. But with just cause, she assured herself, feeling emotion surfacing as hot tears in her eyes at the way she was allowing him to use and manipulate her—unavoidably—now.

She couldn't forget the impact he had made upon her the first time she had seen him standing there in the drawing room of Marcello's villa—the dark excitement of his features, the blazing charm of his smile, the breath-catching power of his smouldering sexuality. Nor could she forget the way he had looked at her with a fire in his eyes that had touched the secret places of her young, untutored body. But there had been suspicion too—that she'd been too inexperienced to recognise—as he'd looked from her to her mother and then back at Riva again, with a hard, concealed intent behind that lazy urbane charm which she had foolishly mistaken for mutual attraction.

His exciting masculinity had blinded her to everything—even the truth—because he had come to vet his uncle's new fiancée under the pretext of merely celebrating Marcello D'Amico's betrothal.

A picture flashed through Riva's mind of the gentle silver-haired man who had captured Chelsea Singleman's heart and who, for the first time in Riva's life, it had seemed, had made her struggling parent perfectly happy. He'd been nearly twice her mother's age, and yet Riva had had no problem with that. Her mother had been head over heels in love with Marcello, and he with her, and Riva had been happy for them both without a thought for how wealthy he was. She'd been only aware and pleased that all the struggles Chelsea had endured throughout her life, her loneliness and her sometimes inevitable depressions, were finally going to be things of the past.

After a celebratory lunch, tipsy with champagne, they had giggled like schoolgirls while strolling arm in arm through Marcello's spectacular gardens, on one of those sultry, halcyon days before the storm broke.

'I've seen the way he's been looking at you,' Chelsea had commented when their conversation had turned, as it always had, to the disturbing subject of Damiano. 'I've seen, all right—and all I can say is that he's trouble, Riva. And I don't mean trouble like your father was. I mean the type most women imagine they want and then wind up regretting with a passion—especially when he tosses them aside for the next easy conquest, as I'm sure a lot of women must have found to their cost.'

As if her mother's words alone had conjured him up, he had appeared on the hot flagstones in front of them.

'Well...Damiano... Or should I call you Nephew?'

His smile for Chelsea Singleman didn't actually touch his eyes, and he seemed to be assessing the mere ten years or so between their ages.

'A little premature, I think.' With that almost detached air— just one of the many things about him that excited Riva—he dismissed the familiar way in which her mother had addressed him. 'I believe Marcello's looking for you. I think he feels he has been deserted.'

Even the mention of her fiancé's name had made Chelsea's eyes light up.

Keen to get back to him, she turned a little too quickly and almost lost her footing on a crack between the stones. Riva's arm shot out to steady her.

Chelsea had giggled, Riva remembered, obviously self-conscious about making a fool of herself in front of a man of such formidable poise and self-possession. 'Come on then, Riva,' she'd encouraged, eager to get away. 'Let's get back.'

'Not you, *signorina.*'

His soft command had been startling, causing excitement to leap wildly in Riva. But more startling had been the dark, warm hand that had suddenly entrapped hers—because that was how it had felt. Like a trap, Riva thought bitterly, wishing she had followed her instincts and fled from the reckless danger she had sensed, which Chelsea had warned her about. But she had been too flattered and too attracted to him, as well as far too inexperienced and swept off her feet, to care.

'I think your mother has had a little too much champagne,' he'd commented, turning from the figure of the older woman tripping back to the villa with her blonde hair billowing out behind her, like her loose white cotton sundress, and Riva had sensed an edge of disapproval in his tone.

'No, she hasn't. She's just happy.' Instantly she flew to Chelsea's defence. 'And if she has, then why not? She's celebrating her forthcoming marriage, after all.' She didn't know why she suddenly needed to feel protective of her mother. 'Don't you approve of anyone being happy?' she challenged him, and then with a sidelong glance at him from under mahogany lashes she tagged on, far more coquettishly than she had intended, 'Don't you like being happy, Damiano?'

She felt the burn of his gaze move over her face and touch the gentle swell of her breasts, just visible above the multiprint gypsy-style blouse she was wearing with a long plain calico skirt, and she felt their tender tips drawing into tight buds.

'Sì. I like being happy,' he breathed, the downward sweep of those thick black lashes unable to conceal the heated desire in his eyes that promised her that what would make him happy would be to tug loose the strings securing her tantalising blouse and show her pleasure such as she had never known. 'And you, Riva? What do you suppose I should call you if your mother marries my uncle? Cousin?' The intimate way in which he enunciated the word, with those visual images already in her mind of him, stroking and arousing her with those long hands, and that voice that was designed for loving a woman, sent molten heat coursing through her veins.

'What do you mean "if"? It's "when", surely?' She exhaled, her cheeks tinged with colour from the feelings he aroused, which were a wild concoction of sexual excitement, indignation and inexplicable unease.

He smiled that lazy smile, the type that made her feel she was drowning in those incredible ebony eyes. Then he was pulling her gently towards him, allowing his lips to brush hers in a feather-light kiss that sent her rocketing senses into overdrive, before he breathed—humouring her, she realised now—in that dark, seductive and oh, so caressing voice, '*Sì*. When.'

That had been the first of many such blissful times when they were alone together, though she'd never fully lost her nervousness with him, amazed as she'd been that such a frighteningly attractive man could be interested in her.

He'd wanted to know everything about her. Where she came from, who she was, what made her tick. No one had ever made her feel so special—or so aware of herself as a woman. But knowing that he would reject her out of hand if he knew the truth, unable to bear it, she had woven a fanciful and glamorous picture around herself, mixing fact and fiction in a story she'd dearly wanted to believe, unaware of how dangerous he was, oblivious to the sensual and deadly trap he had been laying for her.

When he had made a point of extending his visit to the villa, idiotically she'd convinced herself that it was because of her.

'Be careful, Riva,' Chelsea, aware of her excitement, had warned her daughter again.

They'd been in Riva's suite, experimenting with make-up, because Marcello was taking Chelsea out to dinner. She'd looked young and modern and sensational, Riva remembered with a swift sharp shaft of pain. Because Chelsea had borrowed a dress from her that her mother adored.

'I know he's handsome and mature and far more exciting than any of the boys you've brought home, but he's too experienced for someone of your age. I know we might not look so different, but I've been around a bit longer than you have, and I don't want to see my baby getting hurt.'

'I'm not your baby any more, Chelsea,' Riva had reminded her gently. 'If you haven't noticed, I've grown up.'

'I know.' Standing behind her at the dressing table mirror, Chelsea had bent and kissed the top of her head. 'And dangerously dynamic creatures like Damiano D'Amico have noticed it too—and that's what worries me.'

Oh, Mum! Riva mourned now—now it was too late. *If only I'd listened to you!*

'Don't worry. I can handle him,' she remembered telling her anxious mother.

What a misconception! What a joke!

She'd been so far out of her depth she hadn't realised that her feet weren't even touching the bottom any more, that she was playing with a hard, masculine sensuality that was more dangerous than a lethal current. Unaware that there was no safety net to catch her—nothing to stop her from drowning beneath her own stupidity. Because, desperate to keep him from guessing how inexperienced she was, she had woven an illusion of sophistication around herself that had fooled even a man as worldly as Damiano D'Amico.

'You do know what you're doing, don't you?' he had groaned that night in his private rooms, when things had got so out of hand between them, when her hands had stolen inside his shirt and slipped it off his shoulders so that she could see him, touch him, feel the satin of his pulsing flesh that clothed the exciting strength of his body. The night she had allowed him to lead her into the bedroom, realising that unless she admitted the truth there would be no turning back.

Scared by what her boldness had instigated as she'd allowed her hands and lips free rein over his muscular, hair-feathered chest, she'd been even more afraid of his turning away from her in disgust if she told him the truth, perhaps ridiculing her innocence and her lack of sophistication. There was no way she could have suffered the humiliation of that. It would have been too demoralising and degrading, as well as agonizing, to have him reject her. And so, aroused to fever-pitch by his lips and those skilled and oh, so capable hands on her body, when he'd asked her if she was on the pill, she had murmured tremulously that she was.

He had known almost at once, of course, that she had lied, but things had gone too far, and the fire that had raged between them had been too hot and consuming even for his disciplined will.

As pain had made her cry out, she'd heard his groan of rejection, swiftly followed by one of defeat as he lost control.

It had been an experience she could never have imagined. Rivers of sensation had tumbled through every electrified cell in her body, making her cry out again, but this time in ecstasy from the earth-shattering strength of her climax.

He'd waited until she'd slumped back against the pillows, gasping and spent, before rolling away from her with the swiftness of the mistral that blew down from the mountains in winter, and to Riva it had seemed just as chillingly.

'What the devil was all that about?'

Riva recoiled from the white-hot emotion running through his burning question.

'You lied to me! Why the hell did you think you could get away with lying to me?'

He was angry. She couldn't understand how he could be so angry. Not if he loved her! He should have been pleased, flattered...

'I—I didn't think you'd mind.' Reduced by the experience of a lifetime and then his frightening anger, she let slip the charade of sophistication that had resulted in her winding up in bed with him.

'You didn't think I'd *mind*!' On his feet now, he swung

away from the bed, slapping his forehead as he did so. 'My dear, reckless girl... *Mamma mia!* Did you even *think*?'

Shamed by his unexpected reaction, and by how irresponsible he thought her, she covered her small breasts with the sheet and asked candidly, 'Why is my virginity so anathema to you?' And, in view of how gladly she had sacrificed it for him, she murmured, 'Shouldn't you be glad?'

'No, I darn well shouldn't! What did you imagine I would say? "*Grazie, signorina?* That was very generous of you"?'

'Stop it!' She couldn't bear it! Not his mood, nor his angry words, let alone the meaning behind them. He was reducing what they had just done to nothing. No—worse than that—to something sordid, making her feel no better than a whore.

'And what if I've made you pregnant? Had you thought of that?'

Yes, she had, she remembered thinking, but only fleetingly, caught up in too many other emotions—desire, passion, embarrassment, the fear of rejection.

'Do you really think I will have any sympathy with you if you come crying to me in a few weeks saying you're going to have my baby?'

Numbed by the significance of what those last words could only mean—that he didn't love her—Riva couldn't believe he could hurt her any more until, with eyes narrowing into cold, speculative slits, he added, 'Or was that all part of the plan?'

Pain and bewilderment crumpled her forehead. 'What?' She couldn't even follow what he was saying. 'What plan?'

'Is that why you lied to me about being on the pill?' His features were growing harder with every syllable. 'Were you hoping to snare me in the same way your mother has snared poor, unsuspecting Marcello? Was the magnanimous gift of your virginity just one more clever ploy to try and feather your own nest? The older woman takes on the uncle, while the younger little siren makes a bid for the even wealthier deluded nephew!'

Even now Riva winced from the spearing cruelty of his words. He had been using *her*, although she hadn't realised it then, but he hadn't been able to swallow the knowledge that he might possibly have been a victim of the same treatment—which he certainly hadn't been.

'No!' she'd flung back, rejecting every cruel sentence he'd seemed to think it was his right to throw at her. 'And anyway, I *am* on the pill!' She couldn't bear him knowing she had been such a fool—not after his cold and lacerating accusations. 'And my mother hasn't *snared* Marcello. How you can say that?'

Ignoring her wounded question, he said only, 'You were a virgin.'

She gave a miserable little shrug. 'So? I knew I was coming to Italy.' Wretchedly she went on, compounding the lies and worsening the situation for herself in an attempt to prevent him thinking that she was reckless and foolish, and most of all that she might possibly be in love with him. 'Every girl has to start somewhere.'

'So you chose me to initiate you?' He began pulling on his clothes, his body fit and tanned and agile. 'I'm flattered!' His voice, his face and the hard purpose of his actions assured her he was anything but.

'Why not?' She was near to tears but dared not show it, although her voice was so close to trembling that she didn't risk saying any more.

'Well, I sincerely hope I didn't disappoint you! Unless those cries of pleasure to which you treated me were as fake as you are!' He left her then, with his shirt flying open, his angry exit punctuated by the thunderous closing of the door.

A couple of days later her mother came crying to her because Marcello had broken off the engagement. Damiano, it seemed, had had both women investigated, and had convinced his uncle of their unsuitability to marry into the D'Amico family. He had found out about Riva's father, Chelsea's protest marches, her jobs in downmarket pubs and restaurants. Her emotional breakdowns. The flat she had once vacated, dragging a sleepy six-year-old with her in the night, in a hurry, and without paying the rent.

Though she'd never actually disclosed any of this, Riva realised that it was the innocent seeds she had sown in his mind during their long conversations which had nurtured the suspicions he'd already had about them both, and led him to discover all the things that her mother—that both of them—had tried to cover up, or rather wanted to forget.

Riva confronted him about it, shaking with anger and wounded pride, and it was then that he took great satisfaction from calling her a liar. After all, she *was*, she thought, unable to defend herself. The way she had behaved with him, pretending to be sophisticated, experienced, not letting on about her true background, her upbringing.

'You'll excuse me if I'm not too distressed by not seeing the name of my family dragged down by the likes of you and your mother, *carissima*.'

The sarcasm behind his endearment cut into her like a knife as she remembered how tenderly he had whispered it against her cheek, her throat, her hair, when he had been making love to her; when she had thought he meant it.

Her eyes were like dark green pools in the strained, pale structure of her face. 'You used me.' It was difficult hiding the pain behind that accusation.

Some private emotion seemed to flit across the harsh lines of his face, but all he said in a cool, detached voice was, 'And you were very obliging.'

She had to restrain the urge to slap his cruel, handsome face. He'd taken everything else from her—her girlish dreams, her pride, her innocence—and taken the most important thing of all: her mother's happiness. She wasn't going to let him take her dignity as well.

'It seems we both had our agendas,' he stated coldly, when she was too wounded by his cruelty to speak. 'Mine was to uphold and safeguard the reputable name of my family.'

'You're unscrupulous,' she breathed, still unable to believe it, her pained eyes frantically searching his for any small grain of contrition—remorse—for what he had done. But there was none.

His mouth moved in a travesty of a smile. 'Then it seems that we have both been...what is the expression?...tarred with the same brush. Now, if you'll excuse me, I have business to attend to.' And with that closing remark he turned and strode purposefully away from her, taking with him all her love and trust and the foolish fantasies she had dared to weave around him.

She remembered how they had left that afternoon, with only a manservant seeing them off the premises, how Chelsea had sunk into dejection after that. There had been weeks— perhaps months afterwards—when her mother had shown signs of improvement, but Riva's hopes that the woman would eventually recover from her depressions were short-lived.

When she had come back from the shops that day, and tried in vain to wake her pitiful parent, she'd hadn't even needed to ask herself why it had happened.

Damiano! He had ruined her mother's happiness and the pain of it had taken its toll. There was no question in Riva's mind that he was to blame.

She had cried herself to sleep for weeks, wishing she had never set eyes on him, wishing her mother had never met Marcello D'Amico, that she had never been persuaded into going to Italy with her.

Never mind, she thought now, bringing the car to a hurried standstill in front of the house with the brightly coloured sign outside. At least there was one good thing that had come out of that whole miserable period of her life.

CHAPTER FOUR

'MUMMY!'

Riva laughed, her eyes suddenly aglow, her anxious features smoothing into more relaxed lines as she crouched down to hug the little boy who came rushing into her arms.

'I'm sorry! I'm so sorry!' she gasped breathlessly to the young woman who ran the little pre-school and who came following the little boy out of the house, having seen Riva's car draw up. She hated being late.

'That's perfectly all right.' Rounded and motherly, Kate Shepherd was her friend as well as her childminder, with two older children of her own. 'You know I never mind keeping him. He's an angel,' she breathed, smiling down at the small figure, now intent on showing Riva something he was holding. 'It's just that I have to take my mother for her doctor's appointment at six today.'

Apologising again, Riva studied the brightly coloured cutout shapes that had been pasted onto the card. A card for her, she realised, reading the higgledy-piggledy writing scrawled over its shiny surface.

'He made it all by himself.'

Riva's heart swelled as she hugged him again.

This was the moment she longed for every working day of the week—when she could pick up Ben and listen to him chattering on about his day. He was a very sociable little boy, and enjoyed learning through play. Already he seemed to be displaying signs of his father's sharp brain, she realised, her pride in her child's abilities tempered today by the disturbing and unwelcome memory of the scene that had transpired between her and Damiano earlier.

He didn't know—how could he? she thought poignantly—that he had fathered a son.

When she had discovered she was pregnant, her mother had urged her to tell him. After all, he was as responsible for what had happened as Riva was, the woman had reasoned. And even if he didn't want anything to do with her—the truth of that statement had hurt Riva more than she'd been prepared to let her mother know—wasn't it his responsibility to provide for the child he had fathered?

'Whatever you think of him,' Chelsea had made a point of expressing, mistaking Riva's reluctance for indifference, 'he *does* have a right to know.'

Which he probably did, Riva thought now, knowing that her mother's insistence had stemmed largely from all the hardship she had endured herself in bringing up a child single-handed; she didn't want to see her daughter struggle in the same way. But Riva hadn't been able to bring herself to do what her mother had advised.

Damiano had made it clear just what he thought about her when he had as good as accused her of wanting him to impregnate her so she could use him as a meal ticket for life!

Bitter anger stirred in her still from the sting of his brutal remark, but she wasn't going to let it show in front of Ben.

Perhaps her mother had been right, she thought, ruffling the boy's shiny brown hair, but she hadn't been able to face Damiano again—not after what he had done. And she certainly had no intention of ever asking him for anything. He had thought her reckless, calculating, a fortune-hunter. She didn't want the shame and humiliation of having to go crawling back to him and admitting that, on one of those counts at least, he had been right. If she had gone back to him pregnant, he would simply have thought that he'd been right on those other two counts as well—that she was a gold-digger who had planned for it to happen—and so she had determined right from the start that she would go it alone.

Damiano didn't know she had conceived during that hot Italian summer, any more than little Benito Singleman knew of his Italian dynasty—that Damiano D'Amico, one of the wealthiest and most influential men of his generation in Italy, was his father. He hadn't started asking awkward questions yet, but one day he would. And one day she would tell him, Riva determined. But not yet. Because how could you tell an innocent child that his father—the man he should most look up to—was responsible for destroying his grandmother? That she would probably be alive today if it wasn't for him?

'Come on, darling,' she murmured, putting on a bright smile as she led her little son to the car.

Having always slept well, Ben was surprisingly restless over the next few nights, sleeping as fitfully as Riva did. In fact the night before she was due to go to the Old Coach House again, for an early-morning meeting with Damiano, the little boy was so fretful that after several trips to his room to try and soothe him back to sleep Riva woke, startled by the alarm, feeling as though she'd barely slept a wink.

Dressing hurriedly, and fixing a light breakfast for herself and Ben, it took all Riva's efforts to get the little boy up and on his feet, and she felt decidedly guilty when she finally left him at the childminder's, still rubbing his eyes with sleep.

'He might be a bit grouchy today,' she told Kate, as she handed over the grizzling youngster, and was made to feel even worse than she was already feeling when, having rushed back to her car and started the engine, she glanced back and saw that he had started to cry.

'It's all right, Ben. The day's going to fly, and Mummy will soon be back,' she called out through the saloon's open window.

Who was she kidding? she berated herself, with her insides

knotting up as she raced away. Whether he was happy—as he normally was—or fractious and wanting to stay with her as he'd been this morning, it didn't alter the fact that it was still a long day. The only glimmer of consolation she could take from leaving him was in reminding herself that she was doing it so that she could give him a better childhood than the impoverished and unsettled one she had known herself.

It helped, but only a little. It also wasn't doing her any good having to acknowledge that she had been so worked up over having to see Damiano again this morning that she had scarcely been able to spare poor Ben any time at all.

Had she forgotten to leave his coat? No, it wasn't on the back seat. Had she given him his muesli bar? Did he have enough money? Her brain was whirring by the time she reached the Old Coach House, keyed up, shattered, but nonetheless on time.

'Late night?' Damiano quipped, missing nothing as she came into the room at the back of the house, where he was typing on his laptop at the table.

'You could say that,' she retorted, in no mood this morning to take any of his jibes about 'special dates'.

He looked so fresh and vital, in a pale grey suit, white shirt and silver tie, with his thick hair groomed to perfection, falling tantalisingly over his immaculate collar. While all she had had time to do was rake a quick-fix gel through her hair, throw on her clothes, wave her mascara wand over her eyelashes and rush out the door.

'Was it worth it?'

She gritted her teeth to avoid saying something rude. But she said it anyway. 'Don't you have anything else on your mind but my current love-life?'

He leaned back on his chair, surveying her with disturbing directness.

'With you around...' his gaze moved over the black silk tunic she had thrown over a neat black skirt with an insolence that made her mouth go dry '...I must confess to that being extraordinarily difficult, *cara*.'

Growing hot under that masculine regard, and scolding herself for even letting it affect her, she snapped back, 'Let's forget the false endearments, shall we?'

He merely laughed softly in response. 'Ah, yes. I forgot your propensity for always speaking the truth.'

She moved straight past him, intending to get on with the matter in hand—which was to show him the plans she had come up with for her intended design.

'You haven't answered my question.' He meant about her late night being worth it.

'It was stupendous!' she flung at him with a buoyancy she was far from feeling, dumping her briefcase down on the table and tossing back the flap. She hated his taunts and his ridiculous conjecture, hated *him*! And it didn't help her mood in that she couldn't stop worrying about Ben.

Watching her from under his lashes, Damiano didn't like the way her answer had made him feel.

He supposed he deserved it, provoking her like that. He wasn't normally a man who got his kicks out of quizzing a woman over her sexual behaviour.

The truth was he was jealous! Well, not jealous, exactly. *Santo cielo!* That was far too strong a word to describe what he felt about a woman who was not only a gold-digger but who was far too economical with the truth. She did, however, fascinate him, and he had already come to terms with the fact that he still wanted her. Therefore he intended to have her—in his bed, at least. And what he wanted he always got, through sheer determination, hard strategy and unwavering focus.

But who was this man who kept her awake until all hours—even on a week night? He couldn't deny that it made him sick to his gut when he thought of some other fortunate man holding her slim, naked body in his arms, giving her the pleasure he had given her, his masculinity augmented by her petite womanhood.

Despite what he had said about her faking those cries of pleasure, experience alone told him that in that at least she hadn't lied. She had been as out of control as he had been the night he had made love to her. And he had been her first lover. There was no getting away from that.

So who was this man who left her sleepless and pleasured now? Was it serious? Was that why she didn't mind risking her job for him? Or was he just some casual acquaintance for a good-time girl who enjoyed living it up every night?

Such speculation didn't do anything to improve his mood—or his opinion of her—as he pushed himself to his feet.

'What have you got for me?' he demanded, in a voice that could cut through stone.

'I've tried to meet your requirements,' she stated, taking out a folder of her basic designs, trying not to be affected by his glacial tone.

All she wanted to do at that moment was telephone Kate and find out how Ben was, but from the last time she'd been there she knew she couldn't always get a signal on her cell phone through the thick walls of the old building, and she certainly wasn't going to ask to use one of the landlines in the house. No way was she going to risk letting Damiano find out about Ben.

'I've added a different perspective on the electrics for a lady who's getting on in years and might appreciate a little more light,' she told him, pulling out her laptop, her mouse and a few glossy brochures, 'but I think I'll need to do a bit more work on that while I'm here.'

'Do what you like,' he snarled when she'd finished explaining, and left her to it.

She was immensely relieved when he popped his head round the door a little later and said he was going out.

Grabbing her opportunity, as soon as the sound of his car died away Riva raced outside into the sunshine and rang Kate Shepherd on her cell phone.

'He's perfectly all right,' the woman told her reassuringly.

'He's been making things with modelling clay all morning, and now he's having a nap.'

Immensely relieved, Riva went back inside and carried on with her planning. After a while, as it was so pleasant outside, and because a few of the changes Damiano had suggested looked like taking her past lunchtime, she took the tuna sandwiches she had made the previous night and went and found a sunny spot beside a tree in the overgrown grounds of the old manor, her car rug spread out beneath her on the grass.

Ben was all right. She hugged that knowledge to her like a warm cushion as she lay back under the tree with her head resting on her bent arm, wondering what Damiano would say if he knew he had a son.

Tell him, Chelsea had advised, more philosophical about what had happened than Riva could ever be. In view of what Damiano had found out, who could blame Marcello for not wanting to marry her? her mother had said, defending her fiancé. Making excuses for him, Riva thought grievously, because she'd loved him.

But Riva wasn't as forbearing or as forgiving towards Marcello's nephew. Damiano D'Amico was still the cold-hearted louse who hadn't wanted her or her mother to be part of his uncle's life, who hadn't cared about seducing Riva or stealing her heart for his own cold-blooded ends, and then finally ripping it to shreds. Ben might be his son, but that didn't change a thing. Damiano had still ruined Chelsea's life, Riva thought vehemently, and subsequently hers when she had been robbed of her mother. So why should she feel guilty about not telling him? She and Ben were safe and happy as they were. She had no intention of doing anything that might change that through a misplaced sense of duty!

Suddenly she was aware of a shadow falling across her—a long, dark shadow blocking out the sun.

She shivered, noticing that while she had been lying there the tree overhead had shed all its leaves in a damp, decaying blanket all around her. Bare branches were reaching out to her like gnarled dark fingers, getting closer and closer, threatening her, threatening everything she cared about—loved.

Ben!

Terrified, she bolted upright.

'*Spiacente.*' She felt a strong hand on her shoulder. 'I didn't mean to startle you.' The deep caressing tones were incongruous with the harsh images of what she now realised had been just a dream.

'I must have nodded off.' Her hand flew to her temple. 'Oh, gosh! I'm sorry…' What must he think of her? she despaired, feeling doped and headachy. She was tired because of the sleep she had lost last night, but he must think her lazy, a shirker, sneaking off from her job the minute his back was turned.

'It's all right—I'm not your time-keeper,' he said smoothly, those ebony eyes picking up on the sandwich bag with some discarded orange peel inside that testified to her lunch. He stretched out an arm to help her up.

She ignored it and, grabbing the left-overs of her meal, scrambled to her feet unaided. Her heart was thumping just from seeing him standing there, without inviting intimacy with him as well! She had been so keyed up since meeting him again—which was probably the reason Ben wasn't sleeping very well. He had sensed it—and now that bizarre dream only reflected her state of mind.

Automatically she glanced up at the tree, just to make sure it still had all its leaves. It did. The afternoon, though, had turned cloudy and cool.

'Thinking of climbing it, Riva?'

She looked at him quickly, catching that familiar mockery in his voice. 'What?'

'Didn't you and your mother once spend two days in a tree, protesting about the onward march of progress?'

Brushing crumbs off her clothes, Riva cringed, remembering the meal one newspaper had made of the incident, distorting the truth out of all proportion.

'We were trying to preserve a playing field that developers wanted for two fast-food outlets and a car park. One last green area of land where the local children could play and indulge their imagination, run around and get some fresh air, instead of spending all their leisure time stuck behind computers, playing mindless violent games and packing calories!'

'What happened?'

'The fast-food brigade won.' Developers. Capitalists. People like him. She stooped down and grabbed the rug with both hands, shaking it so aggressively that it sent a little shower of crumbs in his direction. 'And before you say anything else, I didn't lie down in front of that digger—I tripped!'

Something like amusement lit those amazingly dark eyes. Or was it surprise, Riva wondered, in discovering he'd been wrong?

Good! she thought trenchantly, before her mortified gaze dropped to his arm.

'What is it?' Damiano enquired.

'You've got a piece of lettuce stuck to your sleeve.' A piece with salad cream on, she realised shrinkingly, as those long steady fingers picked it off, revealing a small grease mark staining the immaculate cloth.

'Do you want me to sponge it off for you?'

'That won't be necessary,' he said with a grimace.

She had started walking back and he fell into step beside her, too big, too close and far, far too disturbing for her equilibrium. 'What I want to know,' he stated, changing the subject, 'is what makes a girl like you imagine she can take on the world. Fight developers—losing battles.'

'As well as seducing wealthy men for every penny I can get?'

His profile was as hard as a cliff-face. Perhaps he didn't like being reminded of just who had been the seducer and for what purpose!

'How did you get into it?' he pressed, clearly refusing to be baited by her sarcasm. 'You look too small and fragile to take on the establishment, Riva. Councils. Huge corporations. And, yes…even me.'

A thread of sexual tension pulled treacherously at her insides.

'What would you prefer I did? Just keep quiet, lie down and let the whole world walk right over me?' Even you, she appended, but didn't say it. Damiano D'Amico, she had long ago accepted, was someone she could never take on and win. 'I didn't *get into* anything, as you put it. Mum never liked injustice.' It seemed wrong calling Chelsea that, as if she was betraying her mother's wishes in some way now that the woman wasn't around to pull her up on it. 'She believed in fighting causes for the underdog, and I went along with her in the beginning because…well, because I just did. I was an adolescent and thought it was good to try and put the world right. Later I tagged along because…' Because Chelsea had needed her, wanted her support, and because she'd wanted to keep an eye on her mother, because she'd always worried about her, been scared that she might go that one step too far. Sometimes, she ruminated, startled to realise the turn her thoughts were taking, it had felt as if she'd been the adult and her mother the child.

'*Si?*' Those keen eyes were studying her pale, strained countenance, expecting her to continue. Eloquent, multi-lingual, with that unwavering self-assurance, she guessed that, unlike her, he would never be lost for words.

'You wouldn't understand,' she exhaled, turning away.

She could see the coach house through the trees, a pleasing blend of gables and sun-washed stone like the manor it used to serve. One day someone would probably destroy that too, she thought, eager to get back to work. To lose herself in her designing and planning and anything else that might take her away—mentally and physically—from the disturbing orbit of the man walking so purposefully beside her, a dangerous mix-ture of strength and oozing sensuality that made her head spin and her legs feel as though they didn't quite belong to her.

'So who is he, Riva?'

'What?'

'The man who steals so much of your sleep at night that you have to catch up during the day.'

A flame of colour touched her cheeks. 'That's none of your business!'

'If it happens when you're working for me, it is.'

Heavens! Why had she been so stupid?

'Don't worry,' she snapped at him. 'The work will get done!'

There was a little gate at the end of the tree-lined path leading to the courtyard, only wide enough for one person to pass through, and she gave a shocked little gasp when he moved with calculated precision to effectively block her way.

'Who is he?' he demanded to know.

'Look...' She swallowed nervously. His hard, obstructive body was a disturbing threat to her equilibrium. 'I'm sorry if you think I've been skiving. I'll take the job home and put in extra overtime if it makes you happy.'

'That isn't good enough.'

Defiance flared in her eyes. 'Well, it's the best I can do!'

'Perhaps I might get the best out of you if I telephone Olivia and insist that you stay here—with me—while you're doing this job for my grandmother.'

She couldn't believe he had the audacity to be saying this.

'Contrary to what you might think,' she breathed, determined to enlighten him, 'Olivia Redwood doesn't have quite that much dominion over me.'

'But I do.'

Riva caught her breath, feeling a tight, tense sensation in her chest.

He was right, she admitted silently. He'd said he wasn't her time-keeper, but he sure as hell could make life uncomfortable if she didn't jump to his every command. And if he did insist on her staying at the Old Coach House, what would she do about Ben?

'And what are you suggesting?' It was taking every ounce of her courage to stand here and face him like this, challenging him when she knew how ruthless he was, when she was about as capable of outwitting him as a sardine was of outwitting a shark. 'That I sleep in your bed?'

His cruel wide mouth curved in a parody of a smile. 'Is that what you want, Riva? I would have thought you'd learned your lesson the first time, but I see that that clearly isn't the case.'

'Don't you dare!' she warned, panicking as strong hands pulled her close—close enough to feel the warmth emanating from the lean, hard length of his body. And yet the only contact between them were those firm, determined hands resting on her shoulders.

'Is that a protest, *cara*? If it is, then I can tell you now that it's only a hollow one. We both know you're a glutton for punishment, don't we?' His breath fanned her hair, warm and unutterably sensual. 'But even punishment, *carissima*, can be sweet.'

He bent his head then, allowing his lips to brush the corner of hers, so lightly the action might not even have warranted being called a kiss. The barest contact of that slightly roughened jaw against hers was more arousing than she could ever have dared to contemplate. That, with those hands that could turn to steel and yet whose touch was spine-tinglingly tender now as they lightly shaped her shoulders, turning her head to mush and her legs to jelly.

A sick excitement trembled through her as his mouth breathed a sensuous path along her hairline, holding her rigid, poisoning her self-respect and every last principle she held dear.

'Let me go.'

He laughed softly, aware from the gut-tight tension in her

and the way her voice faltered that she could no more hide the way he affected her than she could fly.

'Why? Because you can't accept you want me? You're still a liar, Riva, whether you like it or not—to yourself, if to no one else. Admit it, *carissima*, when you tricked me into making love to you, with your feminine wiles and your amazing act of sophistication, you finally bit off more than you could chew.'

Yes, he was right, she thought, despairing with herself, because nothing she had ever fought for in her life was as insurmountable as her battle against this lethal attraction to him.

Refusing to acknowledge that, at least, she murmured, 'I didn't try to trick you.'

'No? Pretending to be experienced and far less gauche than you actually were? But that isn't the case now, is it, Riva? From the way you responded to me the other day I should not be surprised if you could match my own level of expertise. If I remember correctly, you were keen to get started. But has it lived up to all it promised, that loss of innocence you were so eager to sacrifice? I can't say it sits too well on my conscience that I was the one who led you on to that path.'

'Don't let it bother you,' she breathed, wondering what he would say if he knew there hadn't been anyone else since her reckless behaviour with him. 'I'm sure you'll get over it.'

'*Sì, forse*. Maybe. The question is, *cara*, will you? A woman, I believe, always remembers her first lover, and the imprint of my hands are like brands on your body, are they not? Still burning—scorching the life out of you as the memory of your untutored hands on my body still leaches the life out of mine.'

Incredulity widened the green eyes looking up into his. Had she made that much of an impact on him? Despite all his motives? In spite of using her as a pleasurable tool for his own premeditated ends?

Soft laughter fanned her hair as the hand travelling down

her back slipped under her tunic and cupped her small buttocks, pressing her shockingly against him.

'See, *cara*, if you don't believe me.' The warmth of his hand burned through her skirt beneath her tunic, and she closed her eyes so that he wouldn't see the flame that sprang to life in her from the rock-hard evidence of his arousal. 'Small you might be, but we fit superbly, *carissima*. How long will you hold out, I wonder, before you're forced to admit that you want what you had no qualms about taking from me last time. Pleasure—and of the highest order—regardless of the price you had to pay to get it.'

And he alone knew what that price had been!

But he would wear her down if he could. Overwhelm her with his dangerous persona and his heart-stopping promises of paradise—just as he had done before. Only she was much too scarred by her previous involvement with him ever to fall under his spell a second time.

'Not any more, Damiano. As you pointed out,' she added, remembering how this conversation had started, 'there's someone else now, who keeps me far more amused than you ever could!'

She didn't know if she managed to break free, or if he simply let her go.

Back in the house, she spent the next hour or so unable to concentrate—especially when he came in and stood looking over her shoulder while she was working on her laptop on her new concept for concealed additional lighting.

She should have been finished ages ago, she thought, her body tense as cat-gut, every nerve straining, while she willed her jumpy fingers to work over the keys. Her shoulders slumped in relief when he moved away from her and, without saying a word, left the room.

At least she was nearly finished here today! she thought, gratified, reaching for her cell phone to speak to a lighting specialist about the particular fittings she had in mind.

Realising her mistake—she couldn't get a signal, even from

the terrace—she was putting the phone aside when she noticed the display showing *'One Missed Call'*.

A quick scroll to the relevant menu showed that it had been Kate Shepherd.

Ben!

All the worst possible scenarios started racing through her mind. He'd had an accident! Been taken ill! Why would Kate ring her while she was at work unless something was terribly wrong?

'He wouldn't eat his lunch,' Kate told her after Riva had rushed outside into the courtyard to return the woman's call. 'It's probably because he's been so irritable all morning and it's affected his appetite. But I've got a malted milk drink I could tempt him with—at least he'll be getting some protein. I just wanted to check with you that that's all right.'

'Yes, of course,' Riva assured her, weak with relief as her initial worries drained away. 'He isn't sleeping very well,' she went on to remind Kate. He hadn't been for the past few days, and the previous night he'd been awake so long that she hadn't managed to get back to sleep until after four a.m. 'I've got a particularly important job on at the moment that's made me rather edgy. I think I must have passed on those vibes to Ben—which is why he's been so restless at night—but it isn't doing either of us any good.'

'He's probably just unsettled because you aren't your usual relaxed self. Don't worry. He'll get through it,' her friend promised, just as Damiano emerged from the house. 'You both will.'

'Thanks,' Riva uttered, quickly ending the call.

'Problems?' he enquired, those perceptive eyes touching on the way she snapped her cell phone shut, much too unsettling, far too aware.

'Nothing I can't handle,' she said, a little too brightly.

'Is something not going to plan?'

'Everything's fine,' she stressed with her stomach muscles tightening up.

His mouth compressed in wry acceptance. 'Why didn't you use the landline inside?'

The tension in her stomach was like a vice now, squeezing her intestines. 'I prefer to be independent,' she bluffed.

He looked at her quizzically before tilting his chin skywards. 'Even in this?'

It had started to rain since they had come in, a soft yet relentless drizzle that was already gleaming on his thick black hair and dripping from the shrubs that bordered the front of the house.

Grabbing at straws, Riva said, 'I didn't realise it was raining until I came out.'

He didn't believe her, she realised despairingly. She would have to be witless not to realise that.

'Why don't you just admit you were making a personal call—and one you didn't particularly want me to hear?'

'That's your view,' she retorted, swinging away from him. 'Anyway, I hadn't realised there was a law against personal calls.'

'There isn't,' he said succinctly, his soft shoes crunching over the gravel. 'As to my view—I'd be inclined to call it gut instinct, and my instincts are usually right.'

Not to mention his powers of observation as to body language—her defensiveness and how quickly she had reacted in breaking off that call! But her professionalism couldn't look well in his eyes when she'd dashed in almost late for her meeting with him this morning, fallen asleep under a tree and now used up time he was paying her for—or rather the studio—in making private calls.

'Look, it's been a bad few days for me, all right?' she disclosed, in an effort to vindicate herself, coming to a standstill to appeal to the implacable authority in his face. Doing so, though, made her stomach flip, as if she was riding a rollercoaster. Which working for him was—emotionally, at any rate, she thought, raking agitated fingers through her bright damp hair.

She looked feisty, Damiano thought. And tousled, as though she'd only just clambered out of bed.

And with that tunic gaping open, revealing the pale, delicate structure of her throat…

He had to pull his thoughts up sharply to take in what it was she was saying.

'I'm not usually such a mess.' Riva felt herself growing hot under the dark intensity of his eyes. 'But I've got a few problems going on in my life right now.'

He dipped his head in the subtlest of acknowledgments. 'Anything I can help you sort out?' he offered.

As if! Riva thought, smarting from his derisive impudence, and wondering how any man could be so indecently attractive. It was because of him that she and Ben were having such a tough time at the moment, if only he knew it! And if she was stupid enough to let Damiano D'Amico into her life it would only cause more havoc than she was experiencing now.

'I think I can just about deal with it on my own.'

I always have, she thought grievously, without any help from you. Even when her mother had been there to help she had always been concerned over what state of mind the woman might be in—whether her demanding little grandson might be too much for Chelsea to cope with.

As she turned away again that velvet voice came after her, with inexorable authority this time. 'Get rid of him, Riva.'

She stopped dead in her tracks, clutching her phone to her breast, her shoulders pulled back, her spine so stiff she thought it might snap as she pressed her eyelids tight against the emotion she couldn't let him see. He had meant the boyfriend who didn't exist—not the son he had fathered whom he didn't know, whom she was determined he would never meet. Yet the significance of his words took on a different meaning, one that immobilised her with a cruel and tearing speculation.

Would he have asked her to do that if he'd known about her pregnancy from the beginning? Did he think her so far down the social scale—so far removed from the circles he moved in—that it would have come easily to him to dismiss not only her but the child she was carrying? Buy her off with the money to pay for what to him would have been no more than a minor inconvenience?

Emotion turned to hot tears in her eyes, ridiculing her for wanting to believe that he would have been too ethical to act in that way. She had never once considered having an abortion. Not even when her mother—strung with concern for her daughter—had once gently but firmly suggested that Riva might think about that option. A termination had never—ever—been on the cards.

Mortifyingly, he was stepping in front of her, tilting her pain-scarred features with the aid of a forefinger.

'I see,' he said grimly. Because he did. Or thought he did! She was having boyfriend trouble and he wasn't very pleased about it.

She sniffed back a tear, feeling like a drenched clown, with rain dripping off her hair onto her cheeks and her mascara probably running down her face with it.

'You don't,' she berated, pulling angrily away from him.

CHAPTER FIVE

FORTUNATELY Damiano hadn't carried out his threat of insisting that Riva stayed at the Old Coach House, but she hadn't ruled out the possibility that he might.

Strung up as she had been since she had started working for him, she was glad to be able to spend the next few days in the office, gathering information for the materials she would need, working out time schedules for the various jobs, preparing a final brief for Damiano's approval.

The night before she was due for her next meeting with him at the house, however, she was so on edge she couldn't get to sleep, and then Ben had a mild tummy upset to cap it all.

He feels threatened, she thought guiltily, remembering her conversation with Kate, blaming herself as she sat cuddling him, stroking his soft tousled hair.

'I can't get to Mr D'Amico's today,' she called to tell Olivia the following morning, even though Ben seemed a bit better than he had been the previous night. But she'd made up her mind. Her child came first. 'Ben hasn't been well. I can do some work from here, but I've arranged to meet Damiano at the house at ten. I was wondering…' She felt cowardly even suggesting it. 'Could you possibly ring him? Tell him I've rung in sick?'

Fortunately the woman agreed to, keen not to burden her most valued client with the domestic issues of her staff.

Relieved, Riva managed to coax Ben into eating a boiled egg and some toast, cut into soldiers as he liked it, after which he fell asleep on her lumpy settee, still in his dinosaur pyjamas, lulled by the occasional tinkling of the wind chimes which were hanging above the back door, through the archway to her little kitchen.

He felt secure now she wasn't dashing off to work this morning. The knowledge didn't help her to feel any better about leaving him for so long every weekday, even if he was very fond of Kate Shepherd.

But Riva knew all about insecurity. Her father had only come home when it had been preferable to the alternative, and her mother had always had to be somewhere else in order to provide for them. Then, on top of that, there had been the trauma of her mother's emotional breakdowns, which was another reason Riva was so determined to build a career for herself—a secure future—even if Damiano did seem hell-bent on shaking that security at every given opportunity, so that Ben wouldn't have to experience the fears and instabilities that she had known.

Now that he was asleep she went into his room to change his bedspread and popped it into the washing machine. That done, she grabbed the opportunity to take a quick shower, leaving the bathroom door ajar so he would know where she was if he woke up.

He was still sleeping when she came back into the sitting room, having substituted her dressing gown for pale blue jeans and a white T-shirt, and very gently she lifted him up, deciding he would be much more comfortable in his bed.

She was just coming in from hanging the freshly laundered bedspread on the clothesline in her postage stamp of a garden, when the doorbell rang.

'Damiano!' He was the last person she had expected—or wanted—to see standing outside her door.

'The studio telephoned. Said something about you being unwell.'

And he had driven over here straight away to check! she figured, aghast.

'Well?' he prompted, when all she could do was stand there holding the door open in shocked dismay. 'Are you going to invite me in?'

Of course. She had to, she realised, her mind racing, characteristically running a hand through her still damp hair.

Miraculously, there wasn't a toy or anything else lying around to betray her as she showed him into her small sitting room. Thank heaven she had spent a few minutes tidying up!

Reluctantly, though, she noted the impact Damiano's presence made upon her little ground-floor flat. He seemed to dominate it with his height, his sheer masculinity and his dangerous persona. His shoulders were wide beneath the sleek cut of his dark suit jacket, and the spruce of his cologne was making her want to inhale until she hyperventilated.

After a swift survey of the room, those all-seeing eyes returned to Riva, resting on her fresh, unblemished complexion.

She swallowed, feeling exposed by his stripping regard, wishing she'd at least had time to put on some mascara.

'I must say you look rather pale. But then you always do,' he remarked, with that firm mouth twisting speculatively. 'And I think those dark circles under your eyes could testify to far too many late nights. However, Olivia Redwood assured me you weren't well.'

'So you came over to check for yourself!'

His attention was caught by the soft tinkling of the wind chimes above the kitchen door she had left ajar. It was creaking further open, giving her a glimpse of her whirly washing line and Ben's yellow tiger bedspread hanging from it. Fervently, she prayed Damiano wouldn't notice.

'What seems to be the problem exactly, Riva?'

So he hadn't believed her.

'Woman's trouble,' she stated bluntly, hoping to embarrass

him for asking, edging sideways a little to distract his attention away from the kitchen and the washing line. Anyway, it was true in a way, wasn't it? she thought glibly, in an attempt to make herself feel better over misleading him.

He was as unfazed by her declaration as if she had just admitted to having a headache—which wasn't far short of being a reality, strung up as she was from his turning up there unannounced.

'Or man trouble?'

He had obviously got it into his head that she was in some sort of tempestuous relationship with someone, and foolishly she had let him think so, she reflected, regretting it now, because he wasn't prepared to let the subject drop.

'Is this the source of your problems, Riva? The real reason that's kept you away from your work today?'

'I told you why I couldn't come...' Unconsciously she darted a glance towards Ben's bedroom door. 'It isn't my fault if you don't believe me!'

Dear heaven, make him go, she prayed, before her child woke up!

Nothing, though, could make Damiano D'Amico do anything he didn't want to do, she realised with a sinking heart, as clarity lit his eyes and his mouth firmed in grim comprehension when he noted the direction in which her anxious glances were straying. 'Ah, I see.'

'No, you don't!' she snapped, realising what he had to be thinking.

'What's he doing, Riva? Catching up on lost sleep?'

'As a matter of fact he is!' Good heavens! What was she saying? 'I don't know what you think gives you the right to just barge in here—interfering with my private life! I'll be back as soon as I'm feeling better. Now, if you don't mind, I'd appreciate it if you'd just leave.'

He didn't, though. He just stood his ground, his highly polished designer shoes planted firmly on her cheap carpet, his stance intimidating, long legs slightly apart, arms folded across his broad chest, his face an impervious mask.

Any minute now, she thought, Ben was going to wake up. And then where would she be if Damiano realised the truth?

'Why?' Those tanned features hardened inexorably. 'Don't you want him to know I'm here?' He looked as he had that day he had told her he could make life difficult for her—and not only that but enjoy doing it. 'May I remind you,' he imparted with chilling softness, 'that it is probably my money that is keeping you and everyone else in that company you work for employed, in view of the amount of business I put its way. You will do well to remember that. I was beginning to think you were different, but you really are a dishonest little cheat, with a gold-digger for a mother and a convicted fraudster for a father, who thrives on taking any fool for all she can get—only this time, *cara*, this fool knows you far too well!'

'Don't you dare say that!' No matter what he thought of her, she couldn't bear his cruel remarks about the woman who had brought her up. Horrified, she watched him storm towards her son's closed door. 'Where are you going?'

'I think it's time your lay-about boyfriend was acquainted with a few facts!'

'No!' She was chasing after him.

'Why? Afraid he'll dump you if he finds out that we were lovers?'

'Damiano, please…' Impetuously she darted in front of him, blocking the door with her body.

'He means that much to you?' His eyes were glittering like black ice.

She couldn't answer. How could she, she thought, without compounding all the misconceptions he had about her?

'And yet you respond to me with a passion even you can't deny.'

His gaze, falling from hers, burned through her T-shirt with shocking thoroughness. In response she felt the tips of her aching breasts swell into tight, tense buds, betraying her through the soft cotton, letting him know that he was right.

'You want to, but you can't. Isn't that right, *cara*?' One long finger traced the deep vee of her top with insolent awareness, coming to rest beside the small cleft of her breasts just above the place where her heart was beating like the wings of a trapped moth. 'How far would you allow me to go, *carissima*, with the man whose bed you've no doubt not long climbed out of lying there behind that door?'

She pressed her eyes closed to blot out the sight of those arrogant Latin features, to try and banish the sound of that sexily accented voice taunting her, turning her on like no other man had ever been able to turn her on—or ever would. His tangible warmth and that enervating scent of him was making her head spin, robbing her of her ability to reason.

She wanted him! Wanted him to take her in his arms and give her no choice but to allow him mastery over her shamefully willing body. But how could she let him affect her like this after all he had done? When she despised him so much? How could she unless she was depraved—or totally out of her mind?

Hanging on to what shred of her sanity remained, with her eyelids still pressed tight, she got out raggedly, 'I asked you to leave.'

Surprisingly, his hand fell away from her, but there was a triumphant look in his eyes when she dared to meet them again.

'Maybe it would be a pity to destroy his illusions about you, if he's as big a fool as I think he is,' he said grimly, still insulting her. 'No doubt you will resume work at my grandmother's house as soon as you see fit.'

She wanted to retaliate—say something in her own defence—but only the truth could exonerate her, she thought, and she wasn't prepared to tell him that. Besides, unbelievably, he was actually leaving!

As he swung away from her, though, the tiny voice that called to her from behind the door was like a cold hand around her heart. And, what was worse, Damiano had heard it too.

His face as he turned was marked with speculation, puzzlement, disbelief.

The eyes boring into hers held myriad questions, but Riva didn't stay to answer them.

So now you know, you arrogant swine! she thought bitterly, and as the small voice came again she pushed open the door, hurrying to her child's side.

'What is it, darling?'

'I want to get up,' the little boy murmured tiredly.

Not yet, Riva wanted to say, conscious of Damiano standing there in the doorway, judging her, thinking goodness knew what.

It wasn't her son's fault, though, that she was feeling so helplessly in denial.

Gently she said, 'Are you feeling better, sweetheart?' The child nodded, yawning widely. 'Come on, then.'

As he scrambled upright, she plucked the soft blanket off his bed and wrapped it around him, then, with the little boy balanced on her hip, she walked straight past Damiano without a word.

'Why didn't you tell me you had a son?'

Every nerve on alert now, she swung to face him. 'And give you yet another weapon to hurt me with?'

Would he guess? she wondered, her heart racing.

His dark scrutiny rested on the little boy, who was twisting around to stare up at him with wide and fascinated hazel eyes. Would he notice a resemblance? Put two and two together? Why would he? she reasoned with herself. Ben's hair colour was a cross between hers and Damiano's, and he had inherited her pale complexion rather than his father's.

Dry-mouthed, trying to act normally, she declared, 'I need

this job, Damiano. I didn't know how you'd view taking on a single mum to work for you.'

A muscle pulled in his jaw as he glanced from her to Ben and then back to Riva again. 'In a far more favourable way, had you told me the truth.'

Because she had as good as made a fool of him by letting him assume she had a lover, she realised, surprised when she saw the touching smile he gave the little boy.

'What is your name, *piccolo*?'

With unblinking eyes riveted on Damiano, the boy bit his lip, totally overawed.

'It's Ben.' Riva's voice trembled with so much emotion she was sure Damiano would notice it. *Benito*. She slammed the lid down on her desire to say it. 'Ben…' Lovingly she ran a hand over his soft silky hair. 'Say hello to Mr D'Amico.' *Your father*, she knew she should tag on, but couldn't force the words past her lips.

Ben sent up a sheepish grin and said shyly, 'Hello.'

Indulgence laced the deep velvety tones. 'Hello, Ben.'

This first and unexpected interaction between father and son tugged painfully at Riva's heart.

Tell him, she urged herself, remembering her mother's advice, but she couldn't. Even now, when the two of them were face to face, she couldn't.

Swallowing the lump in her throat, she managed to get out, 'I couldn't leave him this morning. He wasn't very well.'

'*Dio mio!*' Concern lined the strong masculine face. 'Nothing serious, I hope?'

Beneath the attention of this stranger, who had obviously made him forget that he had been up half the night, Ben giggled—until self-consciousness overcame him and he turned his little face into Riva's shoulder.

'*Piccolo*…you are not shy?'

He was—sometimes, Riva thought. And then nothing could coax him back to speaking again.

Amazingly, though, a little encouragement from those

caressingly deep tones restored the little boy's confidence almost at once.

Looking back at Damiano, he asked innocently, 'Are you Mummy's new friend?'

If he'd wanted to give Damiano the wrong idea about her, he had succeeded! Riva realised, despairing, as her green eyes clashed with censuring ebony. The man was also probably thinking the same as she was, she thought, with a surprising emptiness inside. Whatever their relationship had been—or whatever it was now—she could never call Damiano D'Amico her friend.

'Mr D'Amico is the man whose house I'm making look nice,' she corrected her son gently, acutely aware of that keen, masculine appraisal of her tense profile.

'Mummy stayed home today,' Ben was telling him importantly.

'*Sì.*'

Those dark, intelligent eyes hadn't left her face. Exposed, feeling as though her nerve-endings were being stripped raw, apprehensively Riva wondered what he was thinking.

'How old are you, Ben?'

It was the question Riva had dreaded.

'Three,' she said quickly, answering for him, hoping the little boy wouldn't contradict her. Bundled up in his blanket, he did look smaller than he really was.

Ben's attention, though, had been caught by the rattle of the wind chimes as the back door blew fully open, revealing his yellow bedspread billowing in the wind. The puffed-out tiger head with its open jaws seemed to Riva to be leering at her, a chasm waiting to swallow her up if she stepped too far off the mark.

'Where is his father?'

This further question, even though expected, produced a sick feeling in the pit of her stomach.

'Ben…why don't you go and switch on your new DVD in the bedroom? It's still in the machine,' she advised, setting him on his feet with his blanket around his shoulders, and was grateful when mercifully he complied.

Without looking at Damiano, she said, 'It didn't work out.'

'That's unfortunate.'

'Not really.' She went over and pulled her son's door to as some helium-filled voices started up their familiar song. 'Ben and I are happy as we are.'

'And was his father just another casual acquaintance passing through your life? Or did this one actually mean something to you?' His tone was scathing, criticising, hard.

Imperceptibly Riva flinched from the reminder of just how 'casual' he thought she had been with him. Hurting, she couldn't help flinging it right back in his face. 'You mean like the one you actually came here to confront today?'

She stormed past him into the kitchen, closing the door to the garden with a rapid jangling of chimes that reflected her mood.

'OK.' He was there, with his hands resting on either side of the archway, as she turned round, impressionably fit and formidably beautiful. 'So in that I was wrong about you.'

'That's big of you!'

He didn't look at all fazed by having to admit that he had made a whopping great blunder in assuming the worst about her. If anything, he looked remarkably contained.

In contrast she felt agitated and uptight as she started putting clean cups and cutlery away, slamming drawers and cupboards in a way she wouldn't normally have dreamed of doing.

'Do I take it that it is Ben who has been on your mind ever since we met?'

Dropping a tea-towel, she hastened to retrieve it—but Damiano had already swooped to pick it up.

'Take it any way you like!' she snapped, snatching it from him.

'So what happened to Ben's father? Were you seriously involved with the man?'

She didn't want this interrogation, but couldn't help retorting, 'I was stupid enough to think so.'

A slight tilt of his head acknowledged the bitterness in her voice. 'What did he do, Riva? Run out on you both?'

Flinging the folded tea-towel down on the work surface, she turned to face him. 'If you must know, I left him.'

She didn't want to talk about it, to remember his verbal brutality, the shame and humiliation she had suffered before she and her mother had been sent away from the villa, the shock of finding out she was pregnant by a man who had merely used her.

'Where is he now?' he pressed, oblivious to how much he was hurting her.

She didn't answer. How could she? she asked herself torturously, finding his line of questioning both unsettling and harrowing in equal measure.

'Does he see his child?'

'No.' *You made it quite clear from the outset that you wouldn't want to!* Before she'd convinced him that there was no chance of her getting pregnant; before reaffirming her bare-faced lie about being on the pill.

'And is that your decision, Riva, or his?'

This last disconcerting question as he followed her back into the sitting room only intensified the guilt already plaguing her.

Angrily she flared over her shoulder, 'Why the third degree? I don't see that it's any of your—'

She clammed up as Ben chose that moment to burst into the room, the film he had been watching still running—abandoned—in his bedroom.

Damiano dropped onto his haunches to take the semi-transparent box containing a plastic dinosaur that Ben wanted him to look at, which Riva had bought for his last birthday. She couldn't help noticing how the muscles bunched in those strong thighs as he inspected the toy.

'You're very interested in dinosaurs, are you not, *piccolo*?' the man observed, tugging at the little boy's blue pyjama top.

'He's been learning about them at pre-school,' Riva told him, desperately wishing that he would go.

'Will you mend it for me?' Ben suddenly appealed to him trustingly.

'No, Ben!' She said it too quickly, much too sharply. 'Mr D'Amico's a very busy man,' she added gently, seeing her son's wounded expression.

Damiano's mouth, however, was faintly mocking. He probably knew what a cost it would be to her pride to have him do anything for her—or for her child.

'What seems to be the problem?' he enquired, pulling the toy out of its box.

'His leg keeps coming off,' Ben supplied.

'We've lost one of the parts,' Riva told him, when it was clear that neither of them could be dissuaded. 'I don't think it can be repaired.'

'Well, let's have a look, shall we?' he said determinedly.

Above those surprisingly gentle hands that were examining the little toy—hands which had loved her with the same tender absorption all those years ago—the masculine wrists furred with dark silky hairs were a striking contrast against the immaculate white cuff of his shirt.

The sight of his dark head bending towards her son's, however, sent another cruel dart into her heart. Every minute that he stayed was weakening her resolve not to tell him the truth…

'Don't you have to be somewhere?' she asked, rather churlishly.

Black hair brushed his collar as he tossed over his shoulder, 'Not particularly.'

Riva clamped her teeth together, willing him to go. Why wouldn't he go? 'No, Ben!'

Distracted by the sight of next door's cat, jumping off the

garden wall, the little boy had bolted into the kitchen, intent on making for the back door.

Riva made a dart for him, but Damiano reached him first. Laughingly, he scooped the infant up into his arms.

'You haven't got any shoes on,' Riva reminded her son gently, in response to his little groaned protest. 'Go and put some on,' she advised more firmly as the man released him, trying not to let Damiano see how much his easy camaraderie with the little boy affected her.

'I wonder where he got that trait from,' he remarked. His gaze slid deliberately to her milky-white feet, with their red-tipped toes curling tensely against the cool lino. 'Some habits never seem to die, do they, *cara*?'

His bittersweet reminder brought the colour rushing to her cheeks.

She had gone barefoot almost continuously during that long Italian summer, and had paid for it when she had cut herself quite badly one day, walking in the grounds with her mother and Marcello.

Damiano had only just come out to join them, looking fantastic as always in dark trousers and a long-sleeved, casually buttoned white shirt that had emphasised the deep bronze of his throat and the crisp black hair of his hard, virile body. Moments later—probably because she hadn't been able to keep her mind on anything else when he was around—she'd stepped on some broken paving.

She remembered her gasped surprise when, having heard her shocked little cry of pain, he had taken one look at her foot and lifted her effortlessly into his arms, unaware of how excited she had been by his breath-catching strength and the thrill of being held so hard against him.

He had carried her down to a stone seat beside an old pump, scolding her gently—first in his own language and then in English—for walking around like a child of nature, he'd said, without any shoes. He'd moistened his clean white handkerchief with fresh spring water from the pump, his strong dark fingers tender, yet disturbingly erotic, around her comparatively pale and slender ankle as he'd ministered deftly to her wound.

What girl wouldn't have fallen for him? she thought poignantly, wondering if his concern for her—his infinite tenderness that day and during the scorching days that had followed—had all been an act.

That way lay insanity, she remonstrated with herself, if she believed that it had been anything but a ploy for his own Machiavellian ends.

He had kissed her, though, afterwards, sitting beside her on that sun-warmed seat, before he'd insisted on carrying her back into the villa. It was the first time he had kissed her, she remembered; the first time anyone had kissed her like that. Open-mouthed, tender and yet overtly sensual, while she had leaned into him and responded with all the eagerness of her awakening womanhood, with the bees and the other nameless insects humming around them, and the scents of erotic herbs filling the heated air.

'It seems you never learn from your mistakes, doesn't it, *carissima*,' he said softly, knowing as surely as she did where her thoughts had taken her.

Which meant what? she wondered, in no doubt that he was referring to more than just her walking about without shoes. Was he referring to the way she still responded to him, even after all he had done? Or to getting herself involved—as he believed—with another man who had supposedly used her? Or both?

'Oh, I've learned, Damiano. Don't be fooled—I've learned,' she assured him brittly. 'You were a very good teacher.'

'I believe in more ways than one.'

With sniping precision she was reminded of how he had accused her of choosing him to initiate her sexually. Crushed, she wondered again what he would say if he knew that there never had been any other man who had shared her bed. That he remained her only tutor in the art of making love—and a bitter lesson she had learned because of it too!

The shrill sound of his cell phone cut through the strained little silence. He reached into his breast pocket, flicked open the slim black casing with a competent hand.

'*Sì. Sì.*' He turned away from her, speaking to whoever it was in his own language.

She couldn't understand what he saying, but the tonal quality of his voice slid like silk across her senses. She remembered how he had used it when he had been making love to her, driving her to fever pitch, uninhibited, wild for him.

'I have to go.' She hadn't realised he had finished the call, and felt herself blushing to her roots, imagining he might have guessed what she was thinking. 'Tell Ben I hope he's feeling better soon...' He was retrieving the toy and the box he had discarded on her dresser when he had gone after the little boy just now. 'And that I'll let him have this back...' he waved it in the air '...as soon as I can.'

'You don't have to do that,' Riva told him, dismayed and surprised to realise he was taking her son's request seriously.

He gave her a calculating smile as he moved over to her, saying with a dangerously smooth quality to his voice, 'Oh, but I do.'

Because then he'd have a reason to come back here, she thought, panicking, scouring her mind for the right words to say that would prevent that happening and finding they just wouldn't come.

'And you, Riva...' A cool finger slid along her jaw, making her breath lock from the frightening excitement even that simple touch produced. 'Openness inspires a far better working relationship.'

'As well as betrayal?'

He didn't stay to acknowledge that breathless little jibe that was torn from her as he let himself out of her flat.

* * *

Damiano's mind was anywhere but on his executive level meeting as he drove straight to his office after leaving Riva.

He had been wrong about her, he accepted, when he had believed that her recent tiredness, her rushing off early and then her absence today was because of some demanding lover. All along what spare time she had was being taken up by the demands of an energetic three-year-old. Who would have believed it? he thought, amazed. Were there any more surprises this girl could throw at him? he wondered, putting his foot down hard on the accelerator to overtake a rather dawdling motorist, aware that the petite little Riva Singleman was taking up far too much of his mental energies of late.

But who was this man she must have taken up with during the months after leaving *his* bed? Was he someone she had hoped to build a life with? Or had he been just a casual lover—someone with whom to amuse herself—as he had been? And if not—if her relationship with this man had been on a far more serious footing—as she had led him to believe—had her child been planned?

Pulling back into the nearside lane, he shot away, leaving the other vehicle standing. He already knew Riva to be a woman who thought very carefully about what she did. The fact that she'd taken steps to protect herself even whilst she was still a virgin was testimony to that. Yet how contemptibly she had spoken of her child's father! he ruminated, checking his rearview mirror. As if she despised the very ground he walked on! Perhaps she did. Perhaps she despised all men, it occurred to him.

He understood now, though, what Olivia Redwood had meant by the hard circumstances she'd said Riva had worked under, and also how hard she must have worked to achieve the standard she had already reached in her career.

It couldn't have been easy, he acknowledged, flicking on his indicator to overtake a cyclist. He was always ready, as the head of a multi-million-pound conglomerate, to commend hard work and dedication whenever he saw it. But it just went to show how focused and self-sacrificing she must be, he found himself thinking, which didn't quite tie in with the little gold-digger he had always believed her to be—the girl who, until this morning, he had suspected of living the high life night after night. That would have been impossible, though—he was forced to recognise it now—even without a child. The serious nature of her job probably still demanded a great deal of studying time.

Something like admiration for her stirred in him for the first time—a sensation that made him feel even worse about the way he had treated her in the past.

He'd had his reasons, he thought doggedly, vindicating himself—though with less conviction than usual—with the reminder that he had done it for Marcello.

He was surprised by how much it angered him, however, to think of Riva sharing her bed with another man. To think that she had surrendered to this man—and who knew how many more?—since she'd surrendered her virginity to *him*.

He laughed harshly out loud at this possessive side of his nature, tormented with images of Riva in another man's arms—lying in another man's bed.

It only strengthened his resolve, therefore, as he brought the Porsche into his company's car park and swung into his own personally reserved space, that the very next man's bed this redhead occupied would be *his*.

CHAPTER SIX

'YOU'RE lucky,' Olivia told Riva a couple of days later as she managed to secure a potential appointment with some decorators in case Damiano approved her brief and the work at the Old Coach House went ahead. 'Things don't always go as easily as planned—especially on your first major assignment.'

No, but all she had to do, Riva was finding, to spur on the assistance she might need, was mention the D'Amico name and problems straightened themselves out like creases under a hot iron. Money meant influence, and influence meant clout. And he had it in bucketloads, Riva thought, resenting him and the power he wielded, even while she nursed a whole heap of guilt about not coming clean to him about Ben.

What was she afraid of? His rejection for a second time? Because he wouldn't just be rejecting her this time, but Ben as well?

From the way he had interacted with her son, it was surprisingly plain that he liked children. But how he would react if he discovered that the common little trollop whom he had bedded and then accused of sleeping with him just to feather her own nest had not only laid but hatched an egg from that nest, didn't bear thinking about. Nevertheless, that still didn't do much to alleviate the feeling that she was being decidedly underhanded in not telling him—a feeling that was only made worse during the lunch he insisted she have with him two days later, under the guise of discussing some changes to the work she was planning to carry out on his grandmother's room.

They barely touched on that subject at all.

'How long is it since you've been on a date, Riva?'

Over her chicken salad, she eyed him warily. He outstripped every other man in the restaurant, she thought, with that air of ruthless confidence, those incredible looks, and that animal restlessness about him that even the dark designer suit couldn't quit tame. 'Is this what this is? A date?'

'No,' he said categorically, making her feel like a fool. 'Of course, if you're hankering after one with me…'

'Most definitely not!'

He laughed softly at the flush staining her cheeks, her staunch denial of wanting any intimate involvement with him. 'How long has it been?' he persisted.

She shrugged. 'Who cares? I don't. And I can't say I've lost much sleep trying to keep a record.'

'Has there been anyone since Ben's father?'

She stiffened, but said casually, 'Not really.' What the heck did it matter if he knew she didn't date? she thought broodingly, noticing the complacency in the firming of that far too sexy mouth. Why should it concern her if he derived some sort of warped satisfaction from knowing that?

'Were you planning to marry him?'

'No.'

'And yet you had a child.'

She looked down at her plate to hide the tension that was suddenly gripping her.

'Wasn't that rather irresponsible?' he remarked.

'This is the twenty-first century, Damiano. Believe it or not, women actually choose whether they want to marry or not!'

'So you chose not?'

'There isn't a law against it, is there?' she snapped, wishing he would drop the subject.

'I just wondered what you do when you have to go away.'

She had often worried about the same thing, but all she said was, 'It hasn't happened yet?'

'But with your job it's likely. Exhibitions. Further training courses. The possibility of working further afield. Supposing a client required you to shoot off to New York or Paris or...?' Those long hands were turned outwards as he shook his head, searching for words. 'Some other such place to assess a particular product he wanted?'

Riva's heart did a double-flip. What was he suggesting? 'Are you saying that would be a problem? That my having a child somehow adversely affects my capabilities and the possibility of who engages me or not?' So Olivia had been right. He *did* frown on the fact that his design manager was a single mother.

He's yours, you bastard!

She wanted to fling it at him, watch his scandalously attractive and arrogant face change when she hit him with it. She had to protect herself, though, from the shame and humiliation of his ever finding out. And Ben. Most of all she had to protect Ben.

Feigning an air of calm, she told him, 'If I could take him with me, I would. If I couldn't, then I simply wouldn't go. If, however, it was absolutely imperative, and I could see no other way to avoid it, then Kate would look after him.'

'Kate?'

'She's Ben's childminder. She's also my friend.'

That angular jaw hardened as he picked up his glass, swallowed the remains of his wine. 'So you'd farm him out?' He set his glass back on the table. 'It doesn't seem the most satisfactory way to bring up a child.'

'I'm not *farming him out,* as you put it!' Riva countered defensively, feeling the bars of two cages of guilt closing around her now. 'Just because you were privileged, you think life's just as hunky-dory for everybody else! Well, it isn't, Damiano. Some of us have to struggle. The rest of us manage as best we can!'

Surprisingly, she was near to tears and, noticing that, Damiano felt a reluctant softening towards her.

It would be so easy to let this lovely young woman get under his skin, he accepted grimly. But that didn't alter the fact that together she and her mother would have stitched up Marcello for every penny he had—he was still certain of that; probably stitched him up too if he had been foolish enough to let himself fall victim to this beautiful redhead's charms. Because he could have done so—and easily—had she but known it.

'I was merely trying to establish how you run your life, Riva,' he expressed quietly, allowing that moment of weakness to pass.

Having put down her knife and fork, not hungry any more, absently she stroked the rim of her plate with her forefinger. 'I didn't know Mum was going to die.' Her chest swelled painfully beneath the white smock top she had teamed with fitted black jeans. 'Naturally it was easier when she was around.'

'Of course.' His tone was surprisingly subdued, even when he went on to remark, 'But somehow I don't see the woman I remember slipping easily into that role.'

Riva's head came up in a bright blaze of colour. 'Because you're so prejudiced towards her. You always were. But she did,' she informed him emphatically, and then, with a greater degree of passion, 'When she was still happy and healthy enough to enjoy it.'

Of course, Damiano thought, feeling the censure that was coming off her in waves. She blamed *him* for bringing about the woman's tragic demise.

Having finished his own meal some time ago, he leaned forward with his arms folded on the table. 'What actually happened, Riva?'

That surprisingly sympathetic note made her look at him enquiringly. There were dark circles under her eyes, and her sadness was so palpable he could almost touch it.

Lowering her gaze, because his was so direct and probing,

Riva took a deep breath. 'She'd always been prone to depression.' There. She had said it. She felt as though a huge weight had suddenly slipped from her shoulders with the acceptance that her mother's own make-up had been self-destructive—even if it did make her feel as though she was letting him off the hook a little by saying it, she thought. But at that moment she was too lost in her regrets to care. 'When I had Ben she seemed better for a while, but then she stopped eating properly—didn't want to get up in the mornings. She also started drinking,' she murmured, so quietly that above the other sounds in the restaurant Damiano could only just make out what she said.

'That must have been hard.'

'Yes, it was.'

She couldn't believe she was opening up to him like this, but perhaps, she considered, it was because he listened. Whatever else he had done, how unscrupulous he was, he *listened*, while often other people were too busy thinking about what they were going to say next to take any real interest in what was being said to them. It was one of the most admirable things she had loved about him—and, as it turned out, the most treacherous.

'She was like my sister rather than my mother, yet she always did what was best for me,' she enlarged fervently, determined that he should know. 'She pushed me every step of the way—with my interests, my education—sacrificing dates, relationships, her own life, so that I could make the most of mine. She was strong in lots of ways, but in others she was… so vulnerable…' She tried to swallow the lump that seemed lodged in her throat. She would never—ever—let him see her cry. 'When she read that Marcello had died, it seemed to push her over the edge.' Painfully, she thought of her once effervescent, impetuous and often girlish parent, comparing her with the despairing wreck of a creature she'd become. 'She loved him,' she concluded fervently, meeting his eyes with such candid opposition that it seemed to bounce back at her from the fiercely intent impact of his.

Emotions were running high. Hers. His. But there were too many harboured passions to be vented over a public table; too many pulsing frustrations that were throbbing for release.

'Let's get out of here,' Damiano rasped, getting up and tossing notes down on the table. Catching her hand, he tugged her unceremoniously to her feet.

He didn't speak as he drove the Porsche with uncustomary speed into the open countryside, his mouth a grim line of determination, his hard jaw cast in stone.

He brought the car to a standstill in a quiet copse some way off the main highway.

What are you doing?

She didn't say it. She already knew. They had unleashed a demon back there in that restaurant, and she had been the one who had turned the lock on its dark, incarcerating cell.

As he leaned across her she knew that he was going to kiss her—knew that she couldn't have prevented it even if she had wanted to.

As his arms came around her and his mouth covered hers she was caught up in a furore of feelings she hadn't known she was capable of.

The rasp of his jaw against hers ignited a fire in her blood; his masculine scent and the hard warmth of his body were things she had known and craved in the darkest corners of her dreams, which now brought her wriggling against him for even closer contact with him.

She didn't want to fight him! Only in the way she knew she could win—or at least reach some amnesty with him—in a mutual enslavement of the senses. Even though it would demean and devastate her—because it would devastate him too, bend him to her femininity, subjugate him in his need for her, and because—dear heaven!—she wanted him to need her! Wanted him to want her as much as she wanted him!

With a betraying sob in her throat, she gave into those

darkest desires, her mouth moving hungrily beneath his, her fingers catching in the thick hair that skimmed his collar to pull him closer to her, holding him there while her eager tongue explored and blended with his.

At her abandoned response he shifted his position slightly, to make it more comfortable for them both, his fingers making short shrift of the few buttons of her top.

A small gasp escaped her as his hand slid inside it and his long warm fingers closed around her breast beneath its lacy cup.

'Damiano...'

One who subdues and tames.

The phrase leaped into her consciousness but she didn't care, because this was what she wanted—what she had always wanted, she accepted now—as he slipped an arm under her slender back to raise the burgeoning tip of one breast to his swooping mouth.

His hot suckling action sent spears of need piercing down through her body, setting her on fire with their sizzling heat and making that most secret part of her slick with honeyed moistness.

He had hurt her the first time, but he wouldn't hurt her now, she thought wildly, her mind racing with the thought of him entering her—possessing her—until she was filled with him: his need, his desire, the pulsing heat of that most intimate part of his body.

But they were in his car...

She gave a raw gasp as his fingers found her other breast, teasing the pale orb at its centre into excruciating sensitivity.

'Damiano, please...'

His soft laughter fanned the upper swell of the smooth pale mound he was fondling. 'Damiano, yes? Or Damiano, stop?'

He didn't, though, and Riva closed her eyes, gritting her teeth against the pure pleasure he was creating for her—a man she shouldn't even have been talking to, and yet whose lovemaking she craved with every weak, betraying cell in her body.

'I hate you,' she breathed laboriously.

'I know.' There was no regret or smugness in his voice, just pure acceptance of how things were.

The sharp, guttural sound she made mocked her defiant little statement as his hand moved across her abdomen, applying gentle pressure as it rested there. Her uncontrolled arousal was a throbbing he could surely feel, she thought hectically, feeling it herself as a tight, tense contracting in her loins, right down to the pulsing ache between her thighs.

His experienced fingers moved across her pubic bone, cupping her femininity, their warmth burning even through her jeans to the small throbbing bud beneath her briefs.

As his mouth closed over hers again she jerked convulsively against him, her legs moving restlessly, her body aching for the ultimate pleasure she craved.

But there were other ways to attain it. He knew it, and he was making it happen for her. Already she could feel the uncontrollable sensations starting to build.

Moving wildly against that sinfully skilled hand, she turned her face into his immaculate collar to stop herself crying out as wave after wave of sensation poured out of her, leaving her hot and gasping and utterly, utterly ashamed.

She couldn't look at him as she moved back to her own side of the car, swiftly began buttoning up her blouse.

'A strange thing, is it not? he commented wryly. 'Hate.'

Apart from a flush across his cheeks he looked coolly immaculate, unaffected in comparison, his white shirt-cuff a stark contrast against the long tanned hand that had pleasured her as he sat there, idly adjusting his rearview mirror.

Perhaps that was why he had parked here and not taken her back to the Old Coach House, she thought suddenly. Because this way he could still retain his command over her—still remain in control.

She despised him in that moment only marginally more than she despised herself.

'I want to go home,' she said stiffly.

Walking to his car from a meeting with his board that evening, Damiano was looking forward to his game of squash.

It had been a long meeting, with some constructive issues thrashed out, but it had been an even longer, seemingly endless afternoon since he had dropped Riva back at the Old Coach House and watched her race indignantly away in her little car.

She professed to hate him, and yet she couldn't stop this thing that was happening between them any more than he could. It had always been there, he thought, if he was honest with himself. This chemistry, or whatever it was that still drove him along avenues he shouldn't even have been exploring. Such was her hold over him—because it *was* a hold, even though he was trying to stay ahead of the game, remain impervious to her particular appeal. And it was an appeal such as he had never known with a member of her sex before. And heaven knew he had known enough!

But there was a naïveté about her, he decided, that seemed at odds with someone who had been involved in relationships— or one at least—and who was also a mother and a very determined career woman. He had to face it. She was an enigma from start to finish.

He had been surprised, too, by the things she had related to him about her mother, painting a picture of someone remarkably different from the money-grabbing blonde who had tried to snare Marcello.

She was challenging his thinking and he didn't like it, he realised, releasing the catch on his car boot to drop his briefcase inside.

They were from different worlds, he reminded himself pragmatically, and with far too much bad history between them. Wouldn't the advisable thing be to let her go? Get on with his life? What could come of anything between them but a whole heap of anger and recrimination when this fierce and mutual attraction had burned itself out?

About to slam the boot lid down, he noticed the box the little boy had given him still there where he had left it. He hadn't had time to look at it since he had dropped it in there the other day.

What was he doing getting involved? he rebuked himself as he picked it up. Would he even have bothered to bring it with him if he hadn't seen it as yet another chance to break through the barriers that Riva had erected against him? As a sound excuse to return to her flat?

His thinking shamed him—especially when he remembered how optimistic and trusting the little boy had sounded when he had asked him to mend his toy.

With the box in his hand now, he got into the car, pulling his tie loose with satisfying relief, unfastening the top button of his shirt.

As he drew the toy out of its box, something else fell out. A little gift tag, he noted, discarding it on the dashboard while he gave some thought to the repair.

That sorted, he replaced the dinosaur in its carton and, remembering the tag, was about to drop that back in too, when something about it caught his attention.

Reading what was written on the reverse side, he sat there staring down at it, immobilised, his mind a maelstrom of bewildered questions, his blood seeming to freeze in his veins.

It was only seven o'clock, but Ben was already sound asleep, Riva realised, gratified, when she peeped in on him. More than a week of sleepless nights had obviously taken their toll. On both of them, she thought, keeping her fingers crossed that this might herald the start of a more relaxed phase for him—if not for her. Just thinking about what had happened in Damiano's car today still made her blush to her roots.

Closing Ben's door quietly, so as not to risk disturbing him, she went and had a leisurely bath—which only made her dwell on what had happened and made her feel worse, if anything, since the warm water relaxed her, making her body respond like clockwork whenever the man entered her thoughts. And that was virtually non-stop as she lay there, too conscious of the tightening crests of her breasts and the ache in her loins that only his possession would assuage.

She had settled down with some needlework in front of the television in her white waffle bathrobe, and was watching her favourite wildlife programme when the doorbell rang.

Guessing it was probably the neighbour who took in the odd parcel for her when she was at work, she turned the television down and went to answer the door.

'Damiano!'

He looked excitingly dishevelled, still in his dark suit, but with the top button of his shirt unfastened and his tie askew. His thick hair was uncustomarily untidy, as though he had been raking his fingers through it, and as he shouldered his way past her without saying a word she could tell that for some reason he was very, very angry.

'Wh-what's wrong? What is it?' she faltered, her expression wary.

As he swung round she could see the livid mask transforming his striking features.

'Exactly when were you going to tell me he's mine?'

'What?' It came out as a squeak, his question driving all her immediate worries about him seeing her undressed and without any make-up from her mind. 'How…? How…?' *How did you find out?* she was trying to say—and knew the second he flung the tiny gift tag down onto the settee.

'"Happy Fourth Birthday…*Benito*!" You even very conveniently supplied the date!'

Riva darted a dismayed glance down at the incriminating little card. It must have been in the box all this time, since

Ben's birthday over a month ago! How could she have been so lax?

She couldn't speak, let alone answer him, as all her worst fears coalesced inside her, etching lines of alarm and anguish across her forehead.

'He's mine, isn't he?' One stride towards her and he was grabbing her. 'Tell me the truth! Go on. Say it!' His hands were hard on her shoulders as he tried to shake the answer out of her. 'For once in your life try telling me the truth!'

'Yes! Yes, he is!' she flung at him, afraid of his pulsing anger.

'Then why didn't you tell me?'

What could she say?

'You even lied about his age—let me believe he was another man's child!'

'I had my reasons.'

'What reasons, Riva? You bore my child, yet you took it upon yourself to deny me the right even to know of his existence! What reason can possibly justify that?'

'Stop shouting! He'll hear you!' Shame mingled with fear and the mind-scorching knowledge that she had been wrong.

'I don't give a damn if the whole blasted neighbourhood hears me! I want some answers, Riva,' he demanded, although he had lowered his voice by a few decibels. 'And I want them now. Why didn't you tell me when you first discovered you were pregnant?' His fingers bit into her soft flesh, making her wince. 'Why, damn you!'

Bitterness marked her tilted glance up at him. 'I thought you knew the answer to that.'

'Which is?'

'When you found out it was my first time you weren't very complimentary about it.'

A nerve leaped in his jaw. No doubt he was remembering how he'd as good as accused her of making love with him in the hope of bringing a paternity suit against him.

'No... Well...' His hands loosened their grip, so that she was able to tug herself free. 'That was how it appeared to me at the time.'

'And of course the high and mighty Damiano D'Amico couldn't be wrong about a thing like that!'

Hard lines scored his face. 'How did you become pregnant? I thought you were taking the pill?'

'I wasn't.'

'So that was a lie too. Just like everything else about you. The oh, so worldly woman act. Your sexual experience. The father you didn't want me to know about.'

'For heaven's sake! I lied! I know I shouldn't have, but I didn't know what else to do. Haven't you ever been ashamed of anything?'

His upper torso stiffened, as though someone had just punched him hard between the shoulderblades.

'That has nothing to do with the fact that you kept the knowledge from me when you found out you had conceived.' His voice was low and controlled as he held his simmering temper in check. 'When he was born—since. Even when I came here the other day. Just how long were you prepared to go on keeping me in the dark? When exactly did you plan on telling our son that I'm his father? Or weren't you? Were you planning on keeping him in the dark for ever too?'

'No! I don't know! I would have told him eventually.'

'When, exactly? When he had grown up and missed out on having two parents? When I had missed out on the whole experience of his childhood?'

'No!'

'And why, when you obviously hate everything I stand for, did you give him an Italian name?'

Did she hate everything he stood for? She didn't know any more.

Heat suffused her skin as his gaze touched on the gaping neckline of her robe. He'd given her so much pleasure in his car earlier that day, but making love was definitely not on his agenda tonight.

'I didn't see why I should let the way I feel about you influence my judgement over what was best for my child,' she answered, pulling the ends of her robe together. 'Just because you thought my family weren't good enough to be part of yours, nothing can change the fact that D'Amico blood runs through Ben's little veins. No matter what you believe, I wanted him to grow up recognising his Italian roots, that he comes from an old and respected—if pompous and stuck up and totally prejudiced—family! The fact that his father thought the other half of his ancestry was trash I was going to keep from him until he discovered it for himself!'

It was clear from the breath that shuddered through his lungs that her point had hit home—and hard.

'You really believe that?' His voice was strung with disbelief. 'That I would turn away my own flesh and blood? My own son?'

Broodingly, Riva said, 'I wouldn't put anything past you, Damiano.'

The bleakness showing through the accusation in her eyes penetrated his defensive armour. Did she despise him so much that she had really believed he wouldn't accept the child they had both created? She would rather struggle to provide for that child alone—deprive his own son of things that were the child's birthright—than come to him for a single cent?

She had asked him just now if he had ever been ashamed, and he had—of course he had. Of the way he had callously and cold-bloodedly used her—a virgin, even though he hadn't realised it until it was too late—to break up his uncle's relationship with her mother. It had been wrong, and because of his actions she had borne him a child—in secret. The shame in having to acknowledge that made him feel sick to his stomach.

The fact was, though, that she *had* kept it a secret and, still in shock, still reeling from being left to find out about it as he had, he didn't think he could ever forgive her for that.

'I want to get to know my son,' he breathed, with every pulsing cell in his body defying her to try and stop him. 'And I'm going to get to know him whether you like it or not. I shan't disturb him tonight,' he went on, remembering then where he should be, and the game of squash he should be playing. For the first time in his life he had forgotten an appointment, let someone down. 'But tomorrow, Riva—I don't care how or when, or how much it hurts that lying little conscience of yours to have to do it, you're going to tell him who I am!'

It was a cool, gusty day, and there were very few people in the park, even for a Saturday.

In the children's play area the only swing in use was the one occupied by Ben.

'It's Mr Mico!' the little boy exclaimed, catching sight of the tall, lithe figure in dark blue shirt and blue jeans at the same time as Riva did. It was the only concession he had granted her last night—that they meet in the park.

Her heart leaped, and her stomach was churning queasily beneath her light jacket and cropped jeans as she caught the swing and Ben went racing off towards the man striding purposefully across the grass.

The little boy reached him before she did, and in spite of their angry confrontation of the previous night something caught in Riva's throat as Damiano swept their son up into his arms.

'So you came,' he observed coolly over the boy's shoulder as she joined them, his eyes hooded, the tautness of his features hiding all the other emotion he must have been feeling.

'What did you imagine?' The wells of her eyes were dark from where she had been lying awake all night, reliving the scene in her flat, worrying about meeting him today.

'With you?' The movement of his mouth was cynical. 'Who

knows?' he breathed raggedly, his face softening as he turned his attention to Ben. 'Well...' Gently he deposited the child back on his feet and, straightening, said, 'Is there not something you wish to tell us, Riva?'

Riva's already churning insides felt as though someone was tying them in knots.

He wasn't helping her. Taking a deep breath and letting it out again, she said, 'This is your daddy, Ben.'

'Benito...' He had dropped down to the little boy's level now, and was tracing the shape of a little cheek with the side of his hand, brushing the wind-blown brown hair tinged with snatches of red back off the infant's face.

'Are you really my daddy?'

'Sì, Ben. I am.' There was no mistaking the crack in the deep Latin voice.

The boy looked up at Riva with his eyes dancing excitedly.

'Does that mean Mr Mico's going to come and live with us? My friend Simon has a daddy—'

'No!' It came out too sharply, and Riva instantly regretted it when the small mouth moved into a disappointed pout. It was much too disconcerting to contemplate, though, with Damiano listening to every innocent but embarrassing word the child uttered.

'Here, Benito.' He handed the little boy a familiar box. 'Perhaps you would like to try it out on the path—see if he walks again.'

'My dinosaur!' He was already pulling it free of its packaging. 'You mended my dinosaur!'

Standing upright now, Damiano smiled indulgently down at Ben. 'Is that not what fathers are for?'

'Look, Mummy! He's mended my dinosaur.'

'Yes, darling. So I see.' Inexplicably moved, she took the empty box from him, feeling grateful. She didn't want to feel grateful. 'Thank you,' she forced past her lips, whilst keeping

her eyes on the little boy who was dashing towards the path
to play with his toy.

'Get used to it, Riva. I'm going to be in my son's life from
here on, whether you like it or not. You've got some making
up to do—to both of us—and you're going to start doing it
as of now!'

'What do you mean?' she challenged warily, shrinking
from the daunting resolve that was marking his face, the tone
of his voice, every hard unforgiving bone in his body.

'I mean I'm going home for a while, and you and Ben will
be coming with me.'

'I can't!' Her mind swam in panic and rising excitement.

'Why not?'

'I just can't.' She was finding it impossible to keep her
weak-willed desire for him under control just while she was
working for him, without the havoc he would cause to her self-
respect and her general equilibrium were she to be marooned
with him under far more intimate circumstances. 'There's the
job I'm doing for your grandmother, for a start.'

'To hell with the job!'

'*What?* After all the hours I've put in?' If he could dismiss
it that easily, just how important had it been to him in the first
place?

'Just forget it,' he advised her harshly. 'I would have thought
even you, *cara…*' he placed scathing emphasis on that endearment '…would have to admit that things have changed
considerably.'

He meant because of Ben. But she couldn't help wondering
if he was referring to what was happening between the two of
them as well. After all, he must have realised since meeting
her again that she could no more resist him now than she'd
been able to five years ago. So had he reckoned on that when
he'd specifically requested her for the job in the first place?

Suddenly, knowing him as she did, she couldn't let go of
the idea that it had all been just a ploy to get her there. But
why? she wondered. Just to get even with her? By trying to

seduce her and make a fool of her for the way she had behaved with him in the past? She thought of how uninterested he had seemed that first morning, when she'd been trying to get a grip on what his grandmother wanted, and the constant changes to her proposals that had kept her coming back.

'Are you sure there was even a job to begin with?' she found herself flinging at him bitterly. 'Or have you just been manipulating me for your own amusement?'

'If I have then it would hardly be more than you deserve, would it?' he suggested, in a tone that was unrelenting, still flaying her for keeping the knowledge of his son from him as she had. 'I would never have found out the truth, would I? If it hadn't been for my determination in bringing you under my roof?'

'Don't you mean under your thumb?' she shot back waspishly.

'Still fighting me, Riva?' he mocked, though there was no humour in his eyes. 'That's going to have to stop in front of our child.'

He was right, but she couldn't contain herself, knowing he had done nothing but use her to satisfy his ego since the day she had first knocked on his door.

'And what do you mean—*your* roof?' she queried pointedly as it sank it. 'I thought it was your grandmother's. I bet you don't even have a grandmother—let alone a French one!'

'A figure of speech,' he responded, sounding impatient, but didn't confirm nor negate her statement regarding his relative. 'For heaven's sake, Riva! Pull yourself together! We have a son, and he should be your first consideration.'

Hot colour suffused her cheeks as she squared her shoulders against this hunk of seething masculinity, who even now still managed to look like the object of every woman's fantasy with those casual clothes emphasising his perfect masculine body and his black hair blowing wildly in the wind.

'He is—and has been for the past four years—I don't need you to tell me!' she shot back, affronted by his suggestion that

Ben was anything but her first priority as she glanced towards the little boy, playing a few metres away. 'Anyway, it doesn't alter the fact that I'm employed by Redwoods—not you,' she reminded him, glad to be able to use that lever to get herself off the hook. 'You might think you're their most influential client, but I'm working with a team on other important assignments, not just on a bogus job for you! Olivia's never going to agree to me abandoning my work just so I can go swanning off to Italy!'

'You presume too much, *cara*,' he said, with that same derisive note in his voice he'd used earlier. 'Especially where I'm concerned.'

She frowned, unclear as to what he meant. Not that she cared!

'You haven't any right to start acting so possessively,' she protested. 'Until now we've managed perfectly well on our own.'

His retort came back like whiplash. 'And whose fault is that?'

Biting her lip, Riva knew she couldn't say anything. She had denied him his paternal rights and now he was getting his own back.

'As for you,' he breathed with a dangerous softness, 'you'll do it, Riva. You owe it to Ben, if not to me.'

It hadn't fully sunk in yet that he was accepting responsibility for his child when all along she had believed the opposite would be true. She should have realised, though, that he was too proud, where family issues were concerned, to do anything other than his duty. The way he had cruelly exposed her and Chelsea Singleman in the belief that he was rescuing his uncle was proof of that.

He was right, she thought. She did owe it to Ben—to both of them—to let them get to know each other, no matter how much she rebelled against the idea of going away with Damiano herself.

'Is your passport up to date?'

She nodded in response to his curt demand, feeling a net closing around her.

'Good,' he said as the little boy ran towards them with his mended toy, his face awash with pleasure. 'We'll be leaving before the week is out.'

CHAPTER SEVEN

THE soft sand was warm between Riva's bare toes, a creamy blanket stretching down to the turquoise sea.

When Damiano had said he was coming home, she had automatically assumed he meant to his home in Italy. It was for that reason—as well as on other equally disturbing grounds like the way his intense masculinity affected her, not to mention leaving her job—that she hadn't wanted to go. Italy was Chelsea, Marcello. And painful pathways that she didn't want to journey down. Memories. Excruciating. Bittersweet. She should have known, though, that a man as wealthy as Damiano would probably have homes all over the world.

This ocean paradise and the large white Colonial house shaded by verdant foliage, set against a forested hillside above its own semi-circular cove, were neutral territory.

Perhaps he had given consideration to that, she thought, in bringing her and Ben here to the Seychelles, so that he could make these first days of getting to know his son as easy as possible for them all. Because there were no ghosts here.

They had been here three days now, and with Ben playing in the garden with his new friend, the five-year-old grandson of Françoise and André, the Seychellois couple who looked after the house, Riva had grabbed the chance of a few moments alone. Even so, this beautiful location, with its clear blue skies and dreamy white beach, weren't doing much to ease her anxieties—particularly about her job.

'I need some time off,' she had told Olivia, two days before Damiano had whisked her and Ben out here. 'I know it's rather short notice, but I've got some personal problems to sort out.' And then, feeling that she owed her boss some explanation— as well as being keen to safeguard the job she had worked so hard for—she had come clean and told the woman that she was having to sort some things out with Ben's father, without actually spelling out who Ben's father was.

'Well, if you must—you must,' Olivia had responded, not looking particularly pleased. 'It's just as well that you've been taken off the D'Amico job,' she'd added—obviously already informed by Damiano that he was shelving the project, Riva realised, still piqued by the way he had used her, although she had refused to let it show. 'Otherwise I might have taken a much dimmer view of the whole thing.'

Now, slipping onto one of a pair of matching sunbeds that a groundsman had put there earlier in the shade of the over-hanging palm trees, Riva sat back against the pale padded cushions and, closing her eyes, tried to relax.

'Dreaming of paradise, Riva?'

With her eyes shooting open, Riva felt her pulses start to throb.

Barefoot, and in light linen trousers, Damiano was coming across the sand, his bronze chest exposed by the equally light shirt he'd left to blow open in the balmy wind.

'I hardly need to when it's within touching distance, do I?' she sent up at him dryly as he drew level with her, and realised from the way his mouth twitched in response how he might be choosing to interpret what she meant. She turned her eyes quickly seaward, her cheeks aflame.

'Now, is this not far better than being in the studio?' he said, reminding her of the resistance she had initially put up to coming here with him as he dropped down on to the other sunbed beside her. 'Or better than taking calls from impatient clients complaining about things which are totally out of your control?' He was leaning back against the lounger and suddenly seemed too close for comfort. Whoever had put the beds out must have decided that their illustrious employer and the young woman he had brought with him would want to be within touching distance of each other, she realised, catching the lemony fragrance of the cologne he had used that morning, with the disturbing sensuality of his own personal scent.

'Or dealing with those who just waste your time?' Sarcasm laced her response, at the way he had engaged her just to satisfy his curiosity about her when he'd had no real intention of using her professional skills at all.

'Don't take it to heart,' he drawled, donning the sunglasses he had taken from the breast pocket of his shirt. 'At least it gave you the chance to test your imagination for a while, and I'm sure the experience you've had with me will have helped to stretch you a bit.'

Riva refrained from retorting that she could have done without any stretching from him. He'd probably choose to put a different slant on it just to unhinge her, she thought despairingly, wondering why every word they uttered seemed rife with sexual meaning.

'And I don't consider it wasted,' he said, slipping his arm behind his head, his shirt falling open. 'It's been a fascinating experience for me, seeing what you can do.'

'Really?' It took all her will-power to drag her gaze from the gleaming musculature of his chest, with its crisp sprinkling of hair, and her throat was aching with the crazy longing to touch it. 'Well, I'm glad I kept you...*fascinated*,' she underlined with a coolness that hid her disappointment and those other, more complex emotions she didn't even want to think about. 'And now that you're done amusing yourself it's a case of, "Don't call us—we'll call you"?'

'*Scusi?*' As it dawned what she meant, he laughed and caught her hand. 'You're so defensive,' he breathed, above the soothing wash of the ocean.

There was a line of spaced rocks jutting out of the blue water, worn smooth by the surf-crested waves.

Fixing her gaze on one shiny boulder, so that she wouldn't have to meet the heart-stopping symmetry of his features, she murmured, 'You annihilate people, Damiano.'

The few moments' silence that followed emphasised the shrill chirruping of some native bird in the lush foliage behind them.

'Is that what I did, Riva? Annihilate you?' The mellifluous note in his voice was as caressing as the warm wind that took a corner of the coloured beach towel she'd spread out on her lounger, lifting it playfully across her shoulder.

'Oh, don't worry,' she uttered, absently pushing it back. 'I'm made of much sterner stuff.' Only she wasn't, she thought hopelessly, scared by how vulnerable she was where he was concerned. In an attempt to hide how disconcerted he made her feel, she glanced over her shoulder towards the house.

It was where Damiano's mother had grown up, she had learned on the plane on the way over—a magnificent house which, with its open architecture, high sloping ceilings and airy verandas, had on her arrival taken her breath away.

'Is Ben inside?' She had heard him earlier, caught his laughter above the deep resonance of Damiano's as they kicked a ball around on the terrace. Already he was forming a strong attachment to his new-found dad.

'Sì,' he assured her, and, seeing her gaze still resting on the house, 'What are you doing?' he enquired after a few moments. 'Redesigning the architecture?'

His amused remark jolted Riva out of her anxious speculation as to whether or not he might insist on an equal say in Ben's upbringing. Or worse...

Consequently, in a voice that was as shaky as it was hostile, she told him, 'If you think I'm wasting my time and effort doing anything else for you, you're very much mistaken, Signore D'Amico.'

'Oh, very formal.' His mouth moved sexily even while he was mocking her. 'You know, you really shouldn't pout like that. It makes you far too desirable.'

'Well...' Her heart was thumping, but she thought it safer to ignore his disturbing remark. She told him, on a sigh that emphasised the depth of her frustration, 'I had lots of great plans for my room.' She'd come to think of her project at the Old Coach House as *her* room. 'I don't expect you would have considered them great, but I was excited by them.'

He shifted his position, angling his lithe body towards her. 'I'm always interested in what excites you, *cara*.' The thumb that brushed her slightly pouting lower lip sent a dangerously delicious shiver along her spine.

'I suppose to you it's just some sort of joke?' she castigated, still annoyed at the devious method he had used to get her under his roof, besides trying to deal with the other, more primal sensations that that simple touch had sent soaring through her blood.

'No, it isn't. Share your thoughts with me,' he invited, looking surprisingly serious.

'Why? So you can amuse yourself with me and while away a few more hours at my expense?'

'If I wanted to amuse myself with you, *carissima*, it wouldn't be in conversation.'

No, she thought, tingling from the sensuality in that deeply accented voice, knowing exactly what he'd meant.

She couldn't see his eyes behind the dark glasses, but she could feel them touching her, feel their heat against the pale skin of her shoulders, penetrating the bright multi-coloured sarong she wore tied above her breasts, and her eyes were drawn to his wide mouth, with its full lower lip, her gaze dropping further to the satin contours of his bare bronze chest and beyond...

The air was alive with their mutual chemistries, so charged that she began to talk quickly, to try and ease the tension between them—gabbling at first, but then speaking more easily as she lost herself in her innovations and unique ideas. The classical fountain she had imagined outside on a mosaic terrace, the Greek theme that would have extended indoors.

He listened without interruption while she rambled on, her face aglow, her eyes shining with enthusiasm.

'This talent of yours. It's bone-deep, isn't it?' he said appreciatively, and for once those strongly sculpted features weren't actually mocking her. 'You come alive whenever you talk about it.'

'Do I?' No one had ever told her that before. Obviously not alive enough for him to actually let her put her skills into practice, she thought, biting back a further dig about it by asking instead, 'Have you never been set on fire by something, Damiano? And before you say the obvious, I mean by something you've really wanted to do.'

'Many times. Otherwise I couldn't have carried my business to where I'm fortunate enough to find myself today.'

'Of course.' She made a resigned little gesture. 'Stupid question.'

'No, it wasn't. A lot of people are unfortunate enough to have to work solely for the financial remuneration. But one has to feel the drive—work from the heart. Otherwise there is not enough soul to keep you sustained for as long as it takes to achieve your personal goals.'

'But you didn't have to start from scratch. Do it all yourself.'

'As you have?'

She hadn't actually intended it to sound like sour grapes, and couldn't find the words to express that before he went on.

'No, I didn't, for which I apologise.' Surprisingly, it sounded as though he meant it. 'But what I've done—what I do,' he amended, 'has often involved elements of risk as well as reward.'

And he didn't just mean financial. She understood enough about him to realise that now.

It was good to be talking with him on a more level footing for once, and, seizing the moment, wanting to hang on to it, she enquired, 'How did you start?'

She had asked him before, five years ago, but in those days she had been too excited by him to take in everything he said to her. Although other things were lodged in her memory for ever. Like how he preferred his coffee—strong, with the smallest drop of milk. How he had been sent to school in England and educated at one of the top universities. Like their mutual taste for jazz—although, if she were honest with herself, she had to admit that she hadn't really taken much interest in it until she'd found out that he did. It had all been part of her desperate need to show him that she was mature and sophisticated, when in fact she had been far too young and stupid, doing—saying—anything to impress him.

He was telling her about his childhood and his parents.

His mother had been born here, the descendant of a family of French merchants who had settled here before Napoleon and Waterloo. She had met his father Miguel D'Amico when he had been visiting the island on business, and had been a guest in her parents' house. When he'd come to the Seychelles again a few months later it had been to make their daughter his bride. She had returned with him to his native Italy where, Damiano said, he had been born the following year.

'I had a series of nannies,' he told her, 'but my parents were always there for me—always there for each other. It's true to say I had everything—that I was privileged. But if you think that privilege goes hand-in-hand with a total disregard for others who are less fortunate than oneself, Riva, it doesn't,' he stated pragmatically, although he didn't enlarge any further upon that subject. 'When my mother died I was eleven years old. My father never actually got over her death. He worked like a demon and played hard for the next year or so. Too hard, as it turned out, when he crashed his speedboat into rocks off the Mediterranean coast during the trials for some race he was planning to enter. I think he was so exhausted by grief and from working too hard that he wasn't as sharp as he might have been.'

'I'm sorry,' Riva murmured, aghast, because he had never

told her that. She realised that on this lovely island he was opening up to her as he never had before—hard as she knew he was.

'It was a long time ago,' he said, as though he no longer felt the pain of losing both parents so young and so simultaneously, but she knew he did.

'I went to live with Marcello and his wife. They treated me as though I was their own son. They never had children of their own. Sometimes they would send me here, to spend time with my mother's parents. Sometimes they would accompany me. My grandparents would have liked me to live with them after my parents died, but it was decided that Italy—the D'Amico business—was where my destiny lay. My aunt died just before I left Oxford, and so when I graduated I shelved any plans I'd been making to go off on my own for a while to go home and support Marcello. I was thrown straight in at the deep end, but I learnt fast and hard.'

'And the rest is history,' Riva declared, already aware of how vastly the name of D'Amico Enterprises had grown and expanded under Damiano's command, to become one of the globally successful forces of its day.

'And, since there is no time for any further history lessons,' he stated, getting to his feet in a few economical movements, 'may I suggest you come inside now and freshen up? And when you have I have a surprise for you, *mia bella*.'

'Oh?' She looked at him, intrigued, but he wasn't saying any more, and so, taking the hand he offered her to pull her up, swiftly she gathered her towel and her book and hugged a secret pleasure to herself when those strong fingers remained clasped around hers all the way back to the house.

Having left Ben and his little friend watching television, with the patient and capable Françoise, Riva came down from the pampering luxury of her own private bathroom which adjoined the huge bedroom she'd been given, to find that Damiano's surprise was the unexpected arrival of someone else.

The whole width of one wall of the imposing drawing room—framed by floor-to-ceiling drapes—was open to the sky, offering a spectacular view through the scented gardens to the milky-white crescent of sand and the azure sea. A very elderly woman in black silk was seated near the window, and looked up as Riva entered, her keen dark eyes and world-worn face unable to disguise the fact that once she had been a great beauty.

Riva's heart leaped as Damiano, who had been sitting opposite the woman, rose to his feet as she walked in.

In a long-sleeved cream shirt and dark trousers, both of which accentuated his powerful body, he looked profoundly male and utterly, utterly dynamic.

'Grandmère.' He was addressing the older woman, whose chair he was standing beside now, speaking French as fluently as he spoke English—as if it were his own language.

A trace of a smile touched his grandmother's lips, Riva noticed. So the lady *did* exist!

'Riva, come and meet my grandmother,' Damiano advised, reverting to English, and from the way his dark gaze rested on her taut features as she greeted the old lady she could tell he was enjoying this immensely. 'Eloise Duval.'

Head cocked, the woman smiled quizzically up at Riva, while remarkably sparkling eyes assessed her red hair and her pale skin beneath the simple beige and black sundress she was wearing, which was already turning gold from the sun. 'You seem surprised, *ma chère*, to see me here. I must confess sometimes to being surprised myself at finding I am still here.'

Riva beamed at the old lady's inverted mockery. She knew she was going to like Eloise Duval.

'I'll appreciate your saying nothing of the Old Coach House,' Damiano warned softly at Riva's shoulder when they were distracted by a maid coming in with a tea trolley.

'Why?' Riva whispered out of the corner of her mouth.

'Because she'd be appalled to discover you were using her house to lure women there under false pretences?'

'On the contrary.' His smile as his grandmother turned his way was timed to perfection. 'Only one woman—and I think my intentions were very clear from the start.'

Fortunately the maid being waved away by a gnarled hand obviated the need for any reply.

'And your son…Benito?' The old lady was looking at Riva now with pointed assessment as the young girl retreated, closing the door behind her. 'He is my grandson's child?'

Riva exchanged a swift glance with Damiano. His handsome face was impassive as he stood there, saying nothing. Behind him the fronds of some exotic potted fern stirred in the tropical breeze. 'Er…yes,,.'

'You seem to have some hesitation in admitting it. I did not expect to find you bashful. I believe it is the custom these days to…what is the expression?…put the wagon before the horse. I'm astonished, however, that Damiano has not told me about you both before now.' She sent him a sidelong glance, before giving her full attention to Riva again. 'You will marry, of course.'

Eloise Duval might appear old and frail, and apparently sweet, Riva thought of the slight figure reclining in what was obviously her favourite deeply cushioned chair, but behind all that frailty and sweetness, she realised, there lurked a will of iron. Amazingly, though, Damiano had spared her the need to make some excuse to his grandmother as to why she had kept his child's identity from him. She was infinitely grateful to him for that.

'I—I…' The woman's direct question about their marrying had her blushing and stammering like a schoolgirl.

'We have no plans, Grandmère,' Damiano asserted, saving her, and behind the fondness in his voice for his elderly relative was a clear-cut message not to interfere.

After that the woman requested that they join her for tea. Riva was glad when Damiano's grandmother took up her offer to pour the beverage and hand round the sandwiches and cakes, but she ate very little herself, owing to the fact that her spirits had suddenly taken a dive.

But why? she asked herself when she was sitting down, toying with a daintily cut sandwich. She didn't want to marry him, did she? They were from such different worlds they might as well have been occupying different planets! Besides, men like him didn't marry girls like her. Girls who lied to cover up where they came from. Girls with criminals for fathers. In his world, like married like. And, as he'd pointed out to her five years ago, upholding and protecting the reputation of his family name was everything. He'd made it plain from the way he had treated her then that she was about as beneath him as a piece of rotten shoe leather! She couldn't even begin to kid herself that he might have changed his opinion now. And from the way he got through his women—women like Magenta Boweringham, who were celebrities and the cream of English society—what chance would *she* have? Of course she didn't want to marry him! So why had that casual remark to his grandmother left her feeling so deflated? So low?

'Damiano…I think I will retire to my room.' She didn't know where the afternoon had gone before Eloise Duval made that statement.

Already on his feet, Damiano stooped down and pressed his lips lightly to the wrinkled brow. 'Of course.'

The gesture touched Riva in ways she didn't want to be touched—as did the gentleness with which he helped his grandmother out of her chair.

'It isn't age, *ma chère*,' the woman directed at Riva, who was trying to rearrange her features into more composed lines. 'It is mere fatigue that makes this old body need to rest so early in the day. I have been visiting friends on neighbouring islands, and I am afraid that island-hopping these days, while still enjoyable, is particularly tiring on these small planes.'

'Of course.' Riva smiled, noticing how Damiano lent a strong supporting arm as they walked to the door, although once there Eloise said something to him in French that made him discreetly withdraw.

'I like her,' Riva said quietly, after he had closed the door behind his grandmother. She still felt dispirited for some reason. Unaccountably depressed.

A rather self-satisfied smile softened his angular features. 'I thought you might.'

'Thanks,' she said, very mindful of the awkward situation he had rescued her from earlier.

'For what? Not telling her how my son's mother preferred not to tell me she had borne my child?' His tone was censuring. He was obviously still angry about it, Riva realised. But if he couldn't understand why she'd kept it from him then that was his problem, she decided. Not hers.

Now, with a jerk of her chin towards the door, she said, 'I didn't believe you—and that just told me, didn't it?' she added on a self-deprecating note.

'About my having a grandmother?' When she didn't reply, he said, 'So you added dishonesty to the list of other sins you hold against me?'

She still didn't say anything. How could she? Riva wondered, when she'd been ready to believe the worst about him because of the past.

'I've never lied to you, Riva,' he stated quietly. 'Whatever else you think I might have done.'

She could sense some constrained emotion in him, and it brought her gaze sharply to his, but nothing showed in the dark, hooded depths of his eyes.

She merely swallowed in response, ridiculously affected by what he had just said, and by that indefinable note of something in his voice that she couldn't quite grasp.

'I think I need some time to myself too,' she murmured, her voice sounding decidedly wobbly, and used that excuse to get away from him.

It felt strange, thinking of them all as a family, Riva thought, one morning when Damiano suggested they have a day out together, when until now it had only ever been her and Ben. But Ben was taking to his father like a swallow took to flying: as if it was a natural and essential part of his life.

She couldn't help worrying, though, about what would happen when they had to go back to their separate lives. Separate homes. Separate jobs. That was if she still had a job by the time she got back to the UK, she thought uneasily, still concerned that by taking an indeterminate amount of time off, and at such short notice, she might be jeopardising her whole career. And what about Ben? How would he feel when his father suddenly wasn't around all the time, as he was at the moment? Or was Damiano planning on being a permanent fixture in his son's life?

Anxiety gnawed at her from the worrying speculation as to whether he might use his immense wealth and power to try and take the little boy away from her. And if he did, how would she fight him? Would the courts automatically grant custody in her favour as she was the child's mother? Or would they listen to Damiano if he tried to convince them that he could provide more adequately for his son?

'Look, Mummy! Look at the spiders!' Ben's excited voice broke into her troubled thoughts.

Shaking herself out of her disturbing reverie, Riva looked up to where he was pointing at the telegraph lines stretching above them. She gasped at the sight of the occupied webs filling the gaps between the wires.

'Oh, Damiano!' She shuddered, and in spite of her worries moved instinctively closer to him. She never had been comfortable around creepy-crawlies. 'Oh, gosh!' Unthinkingly she was grasping his arm. 'They're huge!'

'Don't worry. They're harmless,' he assured her, with an amused movement of his strong mouth. 'And they have as much right to be here as we have. More, probably—since these islands are their indigenous home.'

'Just as long as they remember that, and don't try and move

into ours!' she breathed with another involuntary shudder. But it was the feel of that masculine arm coming around her, of that strong, sinewy body that could please and pleasure and even protect her, she thought, ashamed of needing him for any reason, that was responsible for the sensations now shivering along her spine.

'Are you scared of the spiders, Benito?' How naturally she had taken to calling him that!

'I'm not scared,' the little boy boasted proudly, and with a good deal of noise pretended to shoot them all.

Damiano grimaced. 'It's a...what is it you say? Ah, *sì*! A man thing,' he remembered, and the broad smile he gave the little boy as the child ran up to him squeezed her heart with the need to have him smile at her like that.

She watched him sweep their son—shrieking with delight—high into the air. 'I might have guessed!' she breathed, rolling her eyes. Less than a week and already the two of them were as thick as thieves, she thought, amazed by how well they had bonded. She couldn't help feeling as equally threatened by that as she felt pleased.

They had lunch in a local hotel, and 'Afterwards,' Damiano promised Ben, who had insisted on sitting beside him, 'we are going to see something very, very special.'

'Were you as chummy with your own father?' Riva queried from across the table, as Ben tucked into the largest ice cream she had ever seen him try to demolish. 'Or is it just a secret yearning you have to return to your own childhood?' she said dryly.

His sidelong grin acknowledged that she was probably right.

'The latter certainly,' he responded, with a self-mocking twist to his lips. 'And also the former—being "chummy", as you call it, with my father...' Pain darkened his eyes. From the man's untimely death, Riva decided, rather than anything else, when he answered more sombrely, '*Sì*. Yes, I was.'

Riva stuck her spoon into the smaller dish of chocolate ice cream she had ordered for herself. 'You were lucky.' she said.

'*Sì*,' he said again. 'I was.'

She spooned the ice cream into her mouth. It found a tender spot, making her shut her eyes tightly for a moment until the sensitivity subsided.

'What about you?' she heard Damiano asking with some hesitancy. 'Was there ever a time when—'

'No,' she cut in quickly, before he could ask. 'During all my infancy he was in jail, and when he wasn't—before he died— he only ever came back to us when he needed money.'

'That must have been hard,' he accepted.

'For Mum—it must have been. Where I was concerned, I never really knew him. I only missed what I didn't have—what my friends enjoyed, and what you obviously had with your father. What hurt most was that he abandoned us—even more than what he did in defrauding other people. He left us by getting himself put in jail. When I was a child Mum protected me from that part of it. We never talked about it. If anyone ever wanted to know where he was she simply said he was a navy man and away a lot. It was only afterwards—when I started growing up and people asked me about him, when they knew the truth—that we were instantly bracketed as being in the same ball park. Not quite as good as other people.' She remembered the withering looks, the embarrassment it had seemed to cause, how they had been positively shunned by some people. 'I was so ashamed.'

She stared down at the melting brown mess she had made of her ice cream, unable to look at him, recoiling inside from the elaborate lies she had told him all those years ago, hungry for his approval. He had been one of those people. Prejudiced. Discriminating. Unwilling to comprehend how she felt.

'And how do you feel about it now?'

'Now?' His surprisingly soft query made her glance up briefly before she dropped her gaze again, wondering why he'd even asked. 'I've learned to accept that that was just the way he was—that no one's perfect,' she murmured, trying to convince herself as much as Damiano. 'What he did wasn't a reflection on me or on Mum. He was weak and found it difficult to take responsibility—honour commitment. He had good points too. He must have had, otherwise Mum wouldn't have loved him. She didn't love easily. When she did it was with all of her heart. All of her soul.'

As she loved your uncle.

She didn't say it. She didn't have to.

Blame. Accusation. And above all need. It was all there as she lifted her head, in the clouded emerald of her eyes. A desperate longing for just one word of repentance from him that would help her to understand these dangerous feelings she harboured for him—if not to excuse them entirely.

Across the table their eyes met and held, yet she could read nothing in that unfathomable gaze.

Was he even the tiniest bit sorry for what he had done?

'Benito—no!'

The spell was broken by Damiano's swift endeavour to dissuade the little boy from bashing the remainder of his ice cream with his spoon to see how high it would splash.

Surprisingly, Ben responded immediately to the authority in Damiano's voice, dropping the spoon obediently into his dish.

'I think he's reached his boredom threshold.' Riva grimaced, floundering beneath a tide of mixed emotions.

'In that case I think it's time to change that—don't you, *piccolo*?' Damiano suggested with a complicit wink at Riva, and even the knowledge of sharing secrets with him produced a warm feeling right down to her toes.

She knew what the surprise was, of course, but was as thrilled as Ben when they came out onto a large area of scrubland behind the hotel, where a colony of giant tortoises was ambling in the shade of the palm trees.

A little girl was riding on the back of one of the massive shells, but when Ben ran forward to scramble onto another, whose occupant was obliviously munching away at some vegetation, Damiano pulled him back.

'Those shells are very old—that's why they grow so large—so we must respect that, mustn't we?' he advised Ben gently. 'They were hunted nearly to extinction,' he went on, addressing Riva. 'Their main undoing was the fact that they can live for months without food or water, so they were a favourite diet of ancient mariners. Fortunately nowadays there is a conservation programme in place, which means that they can roam freely and safely all over these islands.' As he spoke he was caressing the smooth curvature of the huge shell that Ben had tried to climb on, encouraging the little boy to do the same. 'It's hard to believe that these placid creatures can live up to a hundred—perhaps a hundred and fifty—years old.'

'A hundred and fifty years!' Ben's little mouth was a perfect circle of incredulity. 'That's older than you and Mummy!'

Both adults laughed, and Riva couldn't help thinking how handsome Damiano looked, with his perfect strong teeth gleaming and the crinkled lines around his eyes softening the noble lines of his face. Under the strong sun, she could see a couple of grey hairs just below his temple, mingling with the midnight-black, which added something to his sophistication. She couldn't take her eyes off him.

'Why do they have shells?'

'Because its shell is its home, Ben,' she heard his father saying through a sudden cauldron of desire and need and wanting. 'It protects it from anything that might try to harm it.'

The little boy's eyes widened. 'Like monsters and things?'

Damiano smiled indulgently. 'No, Benito. Not monsters.'

The child looked up at Riva, and back to his father again. 'Why can't we take our homes with us wherever we go?'

Riva smiled and exchanged glances with Damiano. Sometimes a child asked questions to which there were no easy answers, she thought.

Damiano brought his six-feet-plus frame down to the little

boy's level. 'We do, *piccolo*. It's with us all the time, only you can't see it.'

The little brow puckered. 'Why not?'

'Home is in here, Benito,' Damiano said, pressing his bunched fingers to his chest.

Something tugged so hard at Riva's insides that it took her breath away. She couldn't have answered Ben's question so simply and yet so profoundly if she had tried. She was beginning to understand just how much home and family meant to Damiano D'Amico, and wondered with startling comprehension if that was why he had been so driven to protect Marcello. And in that moment she was struck with the even more startling realisation that she was falling in love with him all over again. In spite of everything, she was hopelessly smitten. Head over heels. Crazy about him. And there wasn't a single thing she could do about it.

CHAPTER EIGHT

'TAKE care with that soft skin of yours, *cara*. Skin as pale as yours is apt to burn.'

Lying face down on a sunbed under one of the large thatched parasols at the poolside, because the sea was too rough for the beach today, Riva quickly raised her head from her crossed arms and saw Damiano standing above her.

In a pair of dark bathing trunks, bare shoulders wide above a tapering chest and tautly muscled waist, he looked magnificent, Riva thought, and everything that was feminine in her was leaping in response to the sight of his muscular hair-covered thighs, and the fact that the silky fabric spanning his hips was doing nothing to conceal his powerful manhood.

Strength and beauty—like the bougainvillaea-draped boulders of granite around the pool, she thought, comparing him with them. A specimen of perfect proportions and disciplined fitness.

He was handing her a tall glass, frosted with condensation. 'I thought you might like something to cool you down.'

That was an understatement!

Half turning to face him, hoping he would think that the flush she could feel burning her cheeks was caused merely by the sun, Riva took the cold glass of peach-coloured liquid that promised to quench her thirst. Yet she knew it would do nothing to slake the hunger inside that his very nearness produced.

'Thanks.' She drained half the glass in one go.

Tanned fingers took it from her, setting it down on the small wicker table beside her. 'Your shoulders are already burning.'

So were her insides! Riva thought, when those fingers—cool from the glass—lightly skimmed across the slightly inflamed area. 'I have warned you that with your colouring you can burn even from the rays in the air.'

'Yes, sir.'

'It's not a subject for amusement. Did you put some sun-screen on?'

'Of course.'

'Not enough, obviously. And I fail to see how you can cover every area successfully by applying it yourself. Why didn't you ask me to help you?' He had picked up the bottle from the table and was already unscrewing the cap.

'I can manage,' she croaked, wondering how she could conceal how much she wanted him if he so much as touched her as she watched the milky fluid pool into the palm of his hand.

'Turn over,' he commanded, sitting down on the edge of the sunbed.

Her awareness of him prickled along every nerve. But refusing to do as he was suggesting would only tell him what he already knew—that she was terrified of this attraction between them and what he could do to her, no matter how much she professed to despise him. And so she complied, glad that her white wet-look bikini, with its halterneck strap and skimpy briefs, was at least more modest than the string version she had been musing over in a shop the day before coming away:

'Relax,' he advised, wise to how she'd tensed the instant his fingers slid across her back.

His touch was as sensual as the sun and the wild sea.

'Where's Ben?' Dear heaven! How could you sound breathless when you were lying still?

'Why? Are you worried he might witness something it's rather ill-advised for a four-year-old to witness?'

'No!' It came out too fast, too sharply, trembling on the sensuous edge of her thoughts.

'You're absolutely right, Riva. Nothing would give me more pleasure than to do what we both want and take you up to my room, but there are far too many important issues to sort out before we grant ourselves that ultimate luxury. However, if it makes you feel less guilty about entertaining such thoughts when he isn't around, André and Françoise took him out in the car with my grandmother. They are not likely to return for some time.'

The imagery his words gave rise to, plus the knowledge that there was time for him to do anything with her—despite what he had said—caused her breasts to swell, their tips tightening in shameless response, producing a contraction of need deep inside her.

'What issues?' She could barely speak, and decided not to add fuel to an already inflamed situation by denying the truth of what he had said. He might just call her bluff by showing her he was right, and she had suffered enough humiliation at his hands already.

'What are we going to do about Benito?'

'What do you mean, "do"?'

'As I said before—a child needs two parents?'

'He has two parents.'

'You know perfectly well what I mean. Would you, for instance, allow me to take him out of the country on my own?'

'No.'

'Why not? Because you don't trust me to bring him back?'

'Why should I?' she challenged, and, even though it hurt like hell to admit it, couldn't help adding, 'When I know you would have preferred anyone but me to be the mother of your child.'

Above the powerful surge of the ocean, she heard him inhale deeply. 'Let's just say that neither of us intended this to happen.' So he accepted it now. 'But the deed is done.'

And if it hadn't been she wouldn't be lying here now, with those excruciatingly skilled hands massaging her heated skin, sliding over the curves of her hips, turning her on even if he wasn't intending to—wouldn't be lying here loving him and feeling so guilty about it, aching for him to love her and not just with his body, she agonized. His absence of any feeling for her was torturing her as much as his cleverly manipulating hands were torturing her into hopeless arousal.

'Relax,' he advised for the second time—misunderstanding, she realised, as he promised, 'I'd never try to break the bond between you and Benito. I was merely assessing how we stand—your concerns. And I have a few of my own.'

'Such as?'

'Such as his education,' he enlarged. 'I want him to have the best.'

Turning her head, she tossed up at him, 'Don't you think I don't want that too?'

'I want him to feel settled.'

'He *is* settled,' she argued.

'He might have been, Riva—after a fashion.' Those fingers had slipped beneath the side strings of her bikini briefs, sensuously working in the cool lotion. 'But I know for a fact that ever since we became involved he hasn't been sleeping. You intimated that much yourself. How settled is he going to be now—torn between the two of us?'

'He won't be torn! You can see him as often as you like.'

'As long as it's on your terms?'

She sucked in a breath as his thumbs lightly skimmed the tight curve of her buttocks. 'I *am* his mother!' She didn't want to be having this conversation with him. She wanted him to do what he had suggested just now and…

'I want you both to come and live with me.'

'Live with you?' Shock made it come out on a squeak.

'*Sì.*'

'As your kept woman?' Shrugging off his hands, she brought herself round to face him, leaning back on her elbows, her small breasts thrust tantalisingly upwards. 'What are you proposing, Damiano? A life of luxury for the little upstart...' she couldn't keep the hurt out of her voice '...in exchange for custody of Ben? With the odd sexual favour thrown in?'

His face was a chiselled rock against the hard blue of the sky. 'May I remind you that he's my son too?' He sounded quietly angry. 'And, no. *Santo cielo!* That isn't what I'm proposing.'

'What, then?'

A particularly strong wave, forced up by the heavy swell of the ocean, crashed over the rocks at the edge of the pool, drenching the tiles beneath the granite boulders on its far side, making her gasp.

'I think we should marry,' he said.

She gazed up at him, bemused, her breasts rising and falling sharply. Yet even while she was left reeling from his unexpected proposal she couldn't tear her eyes away from the hard, amazing structure of his features.

He looked incredible, with his ebony hair gleaming, his forehead and nose proud above a mouth that paid homage to everything that was passionate and sensual. A god of eroticism, as beautiful as the angry ocean—and as cruel.

'I can't.'

A frown knitted his thick eyebrows. 'Why not?'

Because you don't love me! She couldn't say that, of course, because then he would know how hopelessly she had fallen for him again, when she should have learned her lesson the first time; she had suffered so much—been so shattered and disillusioned by his brutal betrayal five years ago.

'There's too much between us,' she parried.

'Like this?' Leaning over her, he very gently touched his lips to the sensitive area of her ear.

'No, Damiano.' His breath against her skin sent shudders

of sensation along her spine, and her hands flew up to hold him off—which was a mistake, she realised hopelessly, when just the feel of that hair-feathered chest had her drowning in her need of him. 'Don't!'

'It's what we both want.'

'It's not what *I* want.'

'No?' He laughed softly, dipping his head lower, his lips unbelievably erotic against the heated gold of her throat.

'Damiano, please…' Her hands were moving of their own volition in powerful response to his warm, muscular strength, making nonsense of her verbal attempts to resist him—to distance herself from all that she was feeling—as he pressed her back against the pillow.

The earth seemed to be tilting on its axis as his mouth descended, covering hers in a kiss that demanded as much as it gave. And against all her efforts to stay immune she was kissing him back, her hands coming up into his hair to hold him fast to her as she responded with a need born out of her longing and frustration.

'*Carissima…*' His voice was as caressing as the warm wind that stirred the palm trees, sighing across her skin with those Latin phrases that turned her blood to molten gold.

She couldn't understand what he was saying—knew only that his voice, when he was making love, to her was the most powerful aphrodisiac she had ever known.

With uninhibited desire her eager hands measured the satin-sheathed musculature of his back and the thrilling contours of his biceps, exploring with unashamed luxury the lean line of his flanks and waist and the more intimate contours of his tight buttocks, glorying in the knowledge of her own power as she heard him draw in a sharp breath.

Without her even being aware of him doing so he had untied the strings of her top, and removing it was now tossing the scrap of material away like unwanted wrapping.

An involuntary little groan of self-consciousness escaped

her when he drew back to admire the small, perfectly shaped mounds he had uncovered.

'You are beautiful, *amore*.'

His lashes were drawn down over his devastating eyes, his mouth full and sensual as he regarded her, and Riva thought that she could never compete with the classical male beauty that made him so desirable to her right then.

'So are you,' she whispered, lying like an abandoned nymph under his smouldering gaze, nipples hard and erect, her abdomen taut from the need that was throbbing down through her pelvis, her flushed face racked with desire.

'Can you deny it now, *carissima*?' His voice was hoarse, those sexily murmured words trembling from the heat of his arousal.

No, she couldn't, she thought, closing her eyes against the electrifying sensations that were pulsing through her veins. She wanted to see him topple. To see him as helpless for her as she was for him. To rip down the last shreds of his iron control.

'Can you not at least admit to yourself that you want me?'

'I want you.' It came out as a soft plea on the scented air.

There. She had said it. Admitted that she had no more immunity to this powerful pull he had on her senses than the tides had to the pull of the moon. And in that admission she knew a heightened excitement from the knowledge that she had just given him licence to do *anything*.

The hands on her ribcage slid automatically to her breasts, and a mind-blowing sensation galvanised her into a gasping creature of mindless wanting as those hands moulded and massaged their aching fullness, his palms hot and slick from the sunscreen he had applied.

Desire held her captive as his mouth rained kisses down her throat, over her shoulders and breasts, before he cupped one of the small white mounds and took the excruciatingly taut peak between his lips.

She cried out from the ecstasy of what he was doing to her, her nails sinking into the cushioned strength of his muscular arms.

'Mmm... You taste good, *mia cara*.'

'That's the cream,' she murmured, still remarkably shy, yet still able to find some humour in the situation.

'Then perhaps I should sample what you really taste like.' His heavy-lidded eyes glittered with sensual promise.

Excitement escalated through her as he tugged at the side strings of her briefs, dispensing with them as easily as he had dispensed with the top, exposing her femininity to his heated gaze.

Shyness and anticipation closed her eyes and yet opened her mind to how still the air was—oppressive, almost, as if the very earth was on Pause, waiting for something to happen. Then she became conscious of the humming insects, the rustle of leaves in the shrubs behind them as a lizard darted for cover, the sea pounding relentlessly against the rocks. She was as fundamental, she realised, as the earth and the sea—a child of nature, designed to do this, designed only for this man's loving.

Very gently he put his hands under her buttocks to lift her, and then did exactly as he had promised, his tongue finding and blending with the sweet nectar of her body until she started to move restlessly against him.

'I could give you what you want now—here—but I promise you, *amore*, I can give you so much more inside.' He smiled indulgently at her soft moan of disappointment as he got to his feet, the evidence of how much he wanted her too raw to hide. 'Don't worry,' he murmured, catching her hand and pulling her up, before wrapping her in a soft white fluffy towel that had been folded on one of the other sunbeds. 'We're going to make this last. Heaven knows!' His breath seemed to shudder through him as his arm went round her and he lifted her off her feet. 'I've waited for you long enough!'

Have you?

What was he saying? That he had craved to hold her in his arms? Ached for her the way she had ached for him? Woken—as she had so often since they had met again—from erotic dreams needing her, his body burning with unfulfilled desire, defying the crucifying self-chastisement going on in his mind?

It was cooler inside as he crossed the hall of the empty house and mounted the sweeping staircase, covering each step with swift, effortless strides.

The blinds were drawn in his room, which overlooked the beach, a cool, sensuous haven with a massive bed dominating the luxurious space.

A sultan's loving chamber for the pick of his harem, Riva couldn't help fantasising, and an elusive thought flitted across her mind as to how many women might have shared his bed, and whether she was to be just another moment's glory for this very virile man with whom she was about to share the most intimate of experiences—despite his proposal. But she had wanted him far too much and for far too long to care.

When he laid her down on the cool sensuality of the coverlet she watched like the sultry concubine she had imagined a few moments ago as he peeled off his swimming briefs, revealing every last inch of his hard and pulsing masculinity.

Even the act of him sheathing himself was a turn on, she discovered, unable to look away, held in thrall by the bronze perfection of his body.

Neither of them spoke, their locked gazes conveying their mutual hunger for each other which was the only communication that either of them needed now.

When he came down to her she took his weight with a small gasp.

'Am I hurting you?' Supporting himself on his elbows, he looked and sounded worried.

Riva smiled and shook her head.

She had dreamed about this for so long! How warm and solid his body would feel covering hers, as it had the first time.

How deliciously his hair-furred chest and limbs would rasp against her softness. And the reality was oh, so much better than she remembered!

'Are you sure?' He still didn't sound convinced. 'Your body is so slender and fragile compared with mine.'

He looked so concerned still that she lifted a hand to his face, tracing with her finger the curve of his high cheekbone, the shape of his jaw, the hard, thrusting prominence of his Adam's apple.

'I promise you won't hurt me,' she breathed.

She was wet for him—so ready—her body molten liquid from the unsurpassable technique of his experienced foreplay.

When he slid into her she let out a shuddering cry of pleasure, moving her body instinctively to accommodate his length.

Hot as the day, she felt rather than saw the first earth-defying flash of electricity against her eyelids, felt the deafening crash of thunder roll across the sky.

They were moving as one, locked to each other as the thickening air and the darkening sky closed in around them, binding them in a world where only scent and sound and unbearably sweet sensation existed.

Lightning ripped across the sky with all the power that was driving them—a power that couldn't be contained or tamed any more than they could contain the storm or tame the turbulent sea.

She was up there with it, Riva felt headily, as sensation piled upon sensation. Flying on the wind, burning brighter than the lightning, riding on the wild power of the storm. And then the climax came, and it was like heaven being opened up to her. The powerful outpouring of his seed drove her into a mindless rhythm of sobbing pleasure only matched by the ferocity of the driving rain.

As the last throbs of her orgasm started to ebb away, and she came back down to reality, she became aware of the deluge—heard it cascading like a thousand waterfalls through the trees, over the boulders, on the roof and into the gullies around the house.

It was as if the earth were crying, she thought, after a build up of all that pressure which, like the tension that had been building between her and Damiano over the past few weeks, had now released itself in an electrifying and explosive crescendo.

Lying there in the crook of Damiano's arm, listening to the rain, she thought of what had transpired outside earlier, and wondered with shameless abandon what André or Françoise would make of the two scraps of discarded bikini lying on the ground if they returned before she could get downstairs to retrieve them.

Saying as much to Damiano, she felt the rumble of contentment in his chest as he pulled her warm, damp body closer to his and replied, 'They will simply know you are exactly where you belong.'

'And where's that?' Her voice trembled as she recalled how easily and sensually he had silenced her after she had refused his proposal of marriage. 'In the master's bed?'

'"In the master's bed?"' he echoed lightly, those hands that were casually caressing her making that flame of wanting leap in her again with surprising rapidity. 'Satisfying the master. As she will be doing from now on, I think.' He was idly massaging her breast, seemingly oblivious to the way it responded to him as he sat up and kissed her lightly on the mouth. 'As the master's wife.'

His arrogant assumption cut through the chains of ecstasy that bound her. 'This doesn't change anything, Damiano.' She was struggling to break free.

'No?' He paused to look at her, lying there with her hair damp and ruffled, her mouth still swollen, emerald eyes still glazed in the aftermath of their torrid lovemaking. 'Are you sure about that, *cara*? I'd say things have changed beyond all recognition. Of course if you need any more convincing...'

Before she could stop him his mouth had swooped to suck on one silently begging breast.

Desire was a cruel betrayer, sending piercing need right down through the core of her being.

Groaning from her own defeat, she complained helplessly, 'You can't have everything your own way.'

Against the pale skin of her breast he laughed softly, sucking harder. 'You like me having my own way.'

Bucking from the pleasure, and then from a determined effort to push him away, she gave a little cry of rapturous defeat when he slid down the bed and parted her thighs to do exactly what he had been doing to her outside.

Now, feeling his thick raven hair against her thighs, driven only by the probing insistence of his tongue, her stomach muscles contracted and the delicious excitement started to build again, leaving her helpless to do anything but give in to the wild ecstasy that was overtaking her as he brought it to its full conclusion, confirming what he had just said about her liking him having his way.

'Admit it, *cara mia*, you're as much a slave to your desire for me as I am for you. Fate planted my seed in you and decreed that we should be together.' He started to get up. 'We'll announce it tonight.'

'No!' Panicking, she shot up in bed, her breasts still unashamedly swollen, their tight peaks rosy from his mind-blowing attentions, and other parts of her tender from the uninhibited passion they had just shared.

From the look on his face as he turned round she guessed that his professional skills would never allow him to be thwarted in closing a business deal—which was what this was for him, Riva thought. Or as good as.

Because when he had sated himself and grown tired of sharing his bed with his son's mother—as he surely would, if his track record with women was anything to go by—what then? she wondered achingly, slipping out of bed and moving over to the window. How could any relationship between them work when he wasn't even in love with her, a girl he'd once considered socially beneath him? Probably still did, she accepted painfully. One to whom he would certainly never have considered giving the illustrious D'Amico name if he hadn't got her pregnant in the first place. And he probably still thought he'd been right in doing what he had in destroying her mother's chance of happiness with his uncle.

Reproaching herself for not only allowing herself to resurrect the feelings she had had for the man who had caused her mother so much grief, but for being unable to stop herself leaping into bed with him at the snap of his fingers, she couldn't now compound those feelings of guilt and self-reproach by sealing that ultimate bond with him—no matter how much it hurt her to refuse him; no matter how much she craved the pleasure of his lips and hands on her body.

How could she, she thought, pulling up the blind, without betraying Chelsea Singleman's memory? She couldn't—not even for Ben's sake.

'I can't marry you,' she said to the dripping garden and the rolling surf tumbling onto the beach beyond.

She heard his harshly drawn breath through the last ravages of the storm that was gradually abating now.

'I think, *cara*—' from the sounds coming from behind her, he was shrugging into a robe '—it would be unwise to make that decision too soon. We have a son. His interests must come first. Think about it,' he advised, and from that harder edge to his voice she knew that it was Ben's and only Ben's interests that concerned him. 'I think you'll eventually see that it is for the best.'

CHAPTER NINE

You couldn't help but like Eloise Duval, Riva decided over the days that followed. She instilled an air of calm in people, which Riva was usually far from feeling with Damiano around.

He was out now, doing whatever fathers did with their sons in their special time together, but ever since the day he had proposed—the day of their uninhibited lovemaking in his bed—her earth-shattering awareness of him had only increased a hundred fold. Yet something between them had fundamentally changed.

If she'd felt that the hostilities that had existed between them before were lessening because of Ben, now—possibly because of her refusal to marry Damiano—they had been replaced by something far more complex and unsettling. A new and different kind of tension, induced by the way he was acting with her—so aloof and distant—which, instead of making her equally indifferent to him, only had the opposite effect.

Clever Damiano! she thought, feeling that tight, tense feeling in her loins that happened whenever she thought about him, even when he wasn't around. He knew how hard it was for her to resist this hot and primal thing between them—even if he couldn't possibly know why—and she suspected that he was determined to keep her simmering nicely, on fire for him, even though it must be equally hard for him, without granting her the release she craved, she realised, until she accepted his proposal.

Unless someone far more celebrated and socially acceptable than she was keeping him satisfied, she mused painfully, aware from a local news report that the Boweringham family yacht had been spotted moored off one of the neighbouring islands. But that earlier tabloid report, with that rather sour grapes attitude the woman had displayed over being dumped by Damiano, wouldn't have done anything to endear her to him, Riva attempted to convince herself, and guessed that she was probably only thinking this way to try and ease her own frustration at the truth of how easily he could leave her alone.

Now, with the nasally French voice of Eloise's favourite singer filling the sun-drenched sitting room, Riva was drawn from her disturbing reverie by Damiano's grandmother remarking, 'You seem very sad, *chérie*. Is it that all is not well between you and my grandson?'

They were sewing together this morning, as they had taken to doing of late, and Riva sucked in a sharp breath as the needle she was using suddenly pierced her finger.

'Why do you ask that?' she enquired, shaken by the woman's powers of observation, rummaging in the pocket of her shorts for a tissue to stem the small bright blob of blood that welled up on her skin.

'Here, *chérie*.' An embroidered white handkerchief was being handed to her. 'You should be more careful.'

'Thanks.' Riva took it gratefully. It smelled of freshly laundered linen and lavender. 'You're always in control, Eloise,' she uttered, admiring that particular quality about her. Just like Damiano, she couldn't help thinking—and felt that insidious tension creeping through her veins all over again.

'Someone has to be,' the woman assured her in her mellifluous French accent. 'I don't like waste—of any kind—and that is what I see: wasted happiness.'

A query darkened Riva's guarded eyes.

'Am I not right? *Oui?* You are keeping him at a distance these days. And yet you are not happy with this decision... *non*?'

Riva's shoulders sagged on a small sigh. 'Is it that obvious, Eloise?'

'To an old lady?' Eloise Duval's lips were pursed as she kept her gaze fixed on the ivory tablecloth she was embroidering. 'There are not many thoughts or feelings one hasn't experienced by the time one reaches eighty. And I understand the look of love in a young girl's eyes when I see it.'

Riva sat back against the cushions of her chair, dropping the small hoop over which a small section of her needlework was stretched onto her lap. 'So it is that obvious?'

'And he wants to marry you, *oui*?'

'Did he tell you that?'

'Not in so many words. Only the lucky few can tell and understand what Damiano is thinking, feeling. I, fortunately, have known him long enough to understand when something isn't going to plan for him?'

Riva pulled a wry face. 'When he isn't getting his own way, you mean.' She tried to dismiss the sensual picture of what had happened when she had said something similar to Damiano that afternoon in his bed, but it refused to go away, tormenting, tantalising, intensifying this screaming sexual tension that she was never free from these days.

'And why is that?'

'He doesn't love me.' It was out before she had time to think.

'Is that so important?' That elegantly mature head was still bent towards the embroidery. 'When he can give you so much more? Security. Loyalty. And more significantly a united and stable home for his son?'

'He's my son, too.' She sounded like a petulant schoolgirl, deprived of the privileges of a favoured sibling. It was just that Eloise's comments seemed to bear out Damiano's lack of feeling for her. But Eloise only meant to be kind, Riva assured herself, with a rather wan, apologetic little smile. 'And it's more than that.'

Resignedly, she picked up the hoop again and resumed weaving a length of golden thread through what would in time become a very large wall-hanging which she had brought with her from England, determined to finish it. It was a labour of love which she had designed herself and been toiling over every spare moment she had—which hadn't been very many, what with her studies and looking after Ben—over the past four years. When it was finished, she had long ago decided, and when she got a lovely new flat, it was going to be the first thing she would hang—framed—on her sitting room wall.

'Is it because of what happened with Marcello and your mother?'

Riva brought her head up sharply, her needlework halted mid-stitch. 'Did Damiano tell you about that?'

A silk-clad shoulder moved with customary grace. 'Only very little. He was reluctant to talk about what had happened between his father's brother and Marcello's bride-to-be. But I recognised your name as soon as he introduced you to me. I found it strange that he hadn't told me he had a son with you, but I've since guessed from the way you behave with him—so…prudently at times—that he didn't know.'

Riva caught her breath, once again amazed by how perceptive Damiano's serene, yet keenly shrewd grandmother was.

'Did he tell you he was responsible for breaking them up?' Her words held more emotion than she would have liked to show.

Casting the tablecloth aside, Eloise took off her spectacles and massaged the bridge of her nose. 'Ah, I see.' In the background, the singer's voice sobbed with melodic poignancy. 'My grandson does not easily admit he is wrong. He seldom makes mistakes, and does not suffer them patiently in others. Therefore he finds it hard to forgive them in himself.' Replacing her glasses, Eloise looked up now. 'Are you still punishing him, child?'

Was she?

The woman's direct question had Riva examining her reasons for not doing what Damiano wanted and agreeing to marry him. Of course she wasn't, she decided after a long moment. But even if she were, wouldn't it be no more than he deserved for his overbearing arrogance five years ago? For the way he had treated her—and particularly her mother? For his pride in never admitting that he'd been wrong in what he had done? And for...

She'd run out of reasons, and so she found it all too easy to throw in another. *For making her love him all over again!*

'Come here, *ma chère.*' A gnarled hand was extended towards her. 'Come. Let me see what you are doing with that pretty yellow thread. I see you are still not wanting to reveal the final picture, *non*?'

'Not until it's complete,' Riva insisted, grateful for the change of topic. Chelsea had always maintained it was bad luck to show anyone a half-finished work—whether it was cross-stitch or a painting. But she did as requested and, gathering up the folded length of her fabric, went and knelt down beside the lady's chair.

'Ah! You are so creative!' Eloise praised, studying the small, painstakingly crafted section that Riva was allowing her to see. 'I am sure your interior design work pleases many if it is done with as much care,' she complimented, having been informed of Riva's occupation, if not of the tactics Damiano had employed to get her to the Old Coach House. 'Perhaps one day you will create something for me?'

'Perhaps.' Riva smiled. The least said about that the better, she decided with a mental grimace.

'And now...if you decide you want a change from this mammoth task you have undertaken... I will teach you the stitch you were admiring on my tablecloth earlier. If you do it as well as you do this—' Eloise's dark eyes were sparkling with appreciation of Riva's painstaking handiwork '—I think you will be my prize pupil, *oui*?'

They were both still laughing when the door opened and Damiano walked in.

Both women's heads turned, their gazes held by the poise with which he moved for such a big man, and by the indisputable power of his presence.

Dressed in blue denim jeans and a short-sleeved pale blue denim shirt that hugged his body, emphasising his tan and the gleaming raven of his hair, he looked, Riva decided, pretty sensational.

His smile for Eloise was warm but fleeting, before his lowered gaze clashed with Riva's.

On her knees before him, with his grandmother's arm across her shoulders, she couldn't stop the panicky feeling that she was being gradually worn down by the Duval/D'Amico will. Persuaded, primed and prepared for him, like some bartered bride-to-be, forced to accept the man who was demanding dominion over her for the sake of the family good.

The fact that it would take very little to accept Damiano D'Amico into her life—and consequently her bed—on a far more permanent basis wasn't doing much for her powers of resistance either. Even now she could feel that part of her that responded so readily to him straining at the tight leash of her emotions, and so hard that it was threatening to snap.

Fortunately the highly charged atmosphere was eased by Ben scampering in and flinging himself at full pelt into Riva's arms.

Laughing, she almost fell backwards. 'Did you have a good day?' she breathed, aching with love for him as she hugged his warm body to her, stroking his sun-lightened hair.

His breathless reply was all about Daddy taking him to the airfield—how Daddy had shown him a little plane he sometimes flew about in, how Daddy had let the roof down on the Porsche when they were stopped outside the ice cream shop. Daddy, it seemed, was a big hit with Benito Singleman.

Over the small head she looked up and met the intensity of Damiano's eyes, and felt another hard yank on her emotions.

He would use her son's affection for him to get her to do exactly what he wanted, she realised, trying to deal with her rampant and raging response to his masculinity. Because even if she denied herself the pleasure she craved by not marrying him, how could she deny Ben the right to a permanent hands-on father?

As Ben tugged away from her, she made to jump up, to stop him scrambling onto Eloise, who was crowing over him in French, but her leg had gone to sleep and she collapsed back onto her knees again. Consequently, Damiano reached him first.

'Go and wash your hands,' he advised, smiling indulgently at the little boy as he plucked him from his grandmother's lap, unaware—or perhaps he wasn't, Riva thought—of the chaos going on inside her, first from that charged exchange of glances a moment ago and now from his exhilarating nearness.

'How are you, Grandmère?' As Ben disappeared, doing as he was asked, that Latin voice lapsed into fluent French, deep and resonant and sexy.

'*Je suis fatiguée*, Damiano.' She was tired. 'But I'm not the one whose well-being you should be enquiring after, surely.'

His penetrating assessment of Riva, who was getting uncomfortably to her feet, made her whole body go as weak as her tingling leg. Since she was braless beneath her clinging white strapless top, he couldn't fail to see the tell-tale signs of her response to him, and she was conscious now of showing far too much creamy thigh beneath her flatteringly cut lemon shorts. Which was crazy, she thought, when he knew every inch of her naked body as well as—if not better than—he knew his own!

'I can see how Riva is, Grandmère,' he remarked, his mouth curling indolently as he diverted his interest from Riva's shamelessly betraying breasts to Eloise. 'I don't need to ask her.'

No, he didn't! she thought, despairing with herself. Any

fool could see how she was. Unfulfilled. Frustrated. Throbbing for him!

He left them then and, watching the play of muscles in his broad back as he made his retreat, Riva felt absurdly rebuffed.

'Love him, *ma chère*.' Eloise advised in a curiously moving way, her sun-spotted hand with its well-worn gold ring resting lightly on Riva's arm. 'Grab the passion,' she breathed, rolling the *r* as distinctly as the dramatic French voice that still sobbed away in the background. 'It is so beautiful while it lasts.'

While it lasts…

Through her dejection from his virtually ignoring her, Riva was startled into realising that Eloise might be referring to herself—that perhaps it wasn't only age and the passage of time that had caused that note of regret—of sadness, even—that Riva had picked up in the woman's voice, in the wistful look in those world-weary eyes. Had her marriage to Damiano's grandfather not been all she had wanted? Had there been someone else in her life? Another lover, perhaps? Because there was no doubt in Riva's mind that Eloise Duval would have been very beautiful.

'I think I'll go and see what my son's up to,' she murmured, unable to take any more emotion for one day and, clutching her hoop with the rest of the loosely folded material, she hobbled after Ben as swiftly as her tingling leg would allow.

Two weeks slid into three, and three was rapidly turning into four, and sometimes, relaxed too much by the warm sunshine and the incredible beauty all around her, by the sheer luxury in which Damiano D'Amico lived, Riva couldn't help worrying that she might be in danger of being pampered into submission, wondering if that was, in part, his intention in bringing her here.

After all, just like her mother, she had had to fight and struggle all her life, and it was hard not to feel tempted to just give up the fight. How easy it would be, she thought, when she strolled into the garden alone on one particular evening, to just give in and allow herself to be "kept" by a man—as a lot of women probably might in her position. Not to have to worry about whether she would still have a job this time next month, or whether she'd be able to pay the rent and still put food on the table.

But she wasn't a lot of women. She was her own woman, she reminded herself fiercely, turning her back on the flower-draped verandas of the magnificent white house with its charm and its opulent staff, and most of all its dark, dynamic resident, determined not to weaken.

The following morning Damiano had to fly to one of the neighbouring islands for a short business appointment, and Riva was surprised when he invited her to go with him.

'What about Ben?' she asked, her heart leaping at his un-expected invitation, although she was anxious about leaving the little boy for an entire day.

'You do it all the time,' Damiano reminded her, but before she could retaliate, wounded by his reference to the way cir-cumstances forced her into leaving her son with a childminder, he said, 'Don't worry,' with his mouth pulling at one corner. 'I've had a little talk with Benito and he's very happy to stay with Françoise and André and his great-grandmother. Also his little friend will be here—' he meant the couple's grandson '—as well as the boy's parents and his two elder siblings, and with Eloise to keep an eye on them all I think our son won't even notice that we've gone.'

'You thought of everything, didn't you?' she chided softly, excited and a little scared by how effortlessly he always man-aged to control things.

And now they were coming in over the sparkling ocean, landing in the tiny plane flown by one of his trusted pilots, and she was glad that in this instance he had.

'What a way to commute!' she enthused, pure pleasure radiating from her face as he helped her down onto the hot and dusty airfield. '*Wow!* It certainly beats the seven forty-five from Charing Cross!'

'Perhaps a little less crowded,' he purred in that sexy, sultry accent, before exchanging a few amiable words with the middle-aged pilot, who was holding the door open for them and grinning at her obvious delight.

It was a change, Riva thought as Damiano handed her into the sleek, air-conditioned limousine that had been left, as obviously instructed, at the entrance to the airfield, to feel relaxed with him today, instead of being so emotionally keyed up, and to be free, for a while, of the festering question that was constantly on her mind. If she refused to marry him, what arrangements were they going to make for Ben?

It was still there, of course, at the back of her mind. But no one could stay worried for long amongst such spectacular scenery, which was every bit as awesome as on their own island.

With Damiano at the wheel—she felt more comfortable being driven by him than by anyone else, she had decided since coming to the Seychelles—she was able to sit back and happily enjoy the beauty around her.

Talcum powder beaches reaching down to a sapphire sea streaked with huge swathes of aquamarine; thatched-roofed houses; hotels on stilts with balconies stretching out over the sibilant ocean. And then there were the flowers—flowers everywhere! The pinks and purples of bougainvillaea cascading like necklaces over rocks and boulders and balconies. Scented star white flowers, whose perfume drifted in through the car window like some exotic aphrodisiac, and other abundant blossoms she couldn't even begin to name.

They visited a primary school—the venue for Damiano's appointment—where children smiled warmly at them, and several of the older ones cajoled him into taking their photograph with Riva when they saw her snapping the bright blooms around the multi-windowed building with her camera.

'Just another of your many merits!' she teased, when they

were back in the car and she was looking at the images he had captured so superbly. She had just found out from the head teacher how he had poured money into the school's recreational facilities, and how he always provided one of his aircraft for the children's special educational trips to neighbouring islands.

She didn't tell him that, though, because he didn't know she knew. She just hugged the knowledge to her and felt her reluctant love for him strengthening as they travelled to wherever it was he was taking her, warming her like the sun bouncing off the gleaming white bonnet of the car.

Business over, he shed the light linen jacket he had worn on the plane, and in his short-sleeved white shirt and light trousers looked as casual as she did in her simple sundress as he introduced her to one of the island's spectacular beaches.

'I came here first with my grandfather,' Damiano said as they walked barefoot, their shoes in their hands, over the virgin sand. 'He taught me to windsurf and scuba-dive during my first summer holidays here.'

'Eloise's husband?'

'Sì. He was fun to be around, but he could be strict too. Perhaps a little too strict sometimes. But, like the D'Amicos, the Duvals had a place in society—a reputation to uphold.'

Which was just as strong in Damiano, otherwise he wouldn't have gone to such great lengths to have her and her mother thrown out of the villa the way he had, Riva reflected painfully, too easily reminded of how insignificant her family were compared with his, and of the yawning chasm that could never really be bridged between them because of her background—the stain on her father's character and consequently hers.

'Were they happy?'

'Scusi?'

'Eloise and your grandfather?'

His thick winged brows came together. 'Why do you ask?'

Riva shrugged. 'Oh, I don't know…just something she said.'

He gave her one of those lazy smiles that always made her stomach muscles curl in on themselves. 'What have you two women been doing?' He still couldn't get over how well the two of them had bonded. 'Exchanging confidences the way only your sex do?'

His unusually easy camaraderie with her today helped her shrug off her unwelcome thoughts as she offered up one of her impish grins. 'Possibly.'

'I don't think it was so much a case of them being happy,' he told her, 'as much as knowing that they were doing what was expected—even demanded of them.'

'By their families?'

He nodded. 'It was a merger of minds, money and companies. In spite of that, however, I believe Eloise loved him very much.'

'And your grandfather?'

She sensed his hesitation before he replied.

'He tried, I think. But he was planning to marry someone else before circumstances—and his family—forced him into marrying Eloise. I don't think he ever really forgave his parents or forgot his real love. I think as a young man he probably made the best of his marriage. He was certainly a loyal and supportive husband—in practice, if not always in his heart—and he was a good father to his daughter, my mother. He was never a demonstrative man—certainly not in all the years I knew him. My mother used to joke that she had just "happened", but I was too young at the time to understand fully what she meant. Later I was to realise that my grandparents' marriage lacked…'

'Passion?'

'*Sì.* The grand passion.'

As ours would after a while, Damiano, Riva thought desolately. When you realise that this physical thing you feel for me now isn't enough to sustain a marriage. When you regret

giving up the good life and all those society women for someone you'd be ashamed of anyone scrutinising too closely.

'Poor Eloise.'

It was only when he threw out his hands in a typically
Italian way and exclaimed, 'She is happy! Which is more, I
think, than can be said for you, *amore*,' that she realised she
had spoken aloud. Tilting her chin with the aid of a finger, he
said softly, 'What is it, Riva? Why do you look so sad?'

She wanted to lean into him, to respond to the tenderness
in his voice—in his touch—close the hair's breadth that sepa-
rated them and draw sustenance from his hard lean body. But
she didn't. To abandon herself to him now would make his
withdrawal from her so much more painful when it came—as
it surely would, she realised. As it had for Eloise, when her
husband had discovered that mere duty wasn't strong enough
to keep him interested—no matter how much love there was
on the part of his adoring young wife.

When he leaned forward and kissed her lightly on the forehead she closed her eyes, because being this close to him was
almost too much to bear.

'Come on,' he whispered, taking her hand in the dark,
warm strength of his. 'The day isn't over yet, and we have
still so much more to do.'

CHAPTER TEN

THEY had lunch in a thatched-roof open-air restaurant overlooking another of the amazing beaches—a meal of fresh lobster and tropical fruit and some exotic, non-alcoholic punch that still managed to make Riva feel as though she was floating on air.

Because she was, she thought, just from being with him today.

Afterwards, passing a trackside vendor, Damiano indulged her while she insisted on doing the touristy thing and drank milk from a freshly picked coconut, before whisking her off to a forested valley to find a tree that grew nowhere else in the world.

'So that's it.' Riva gazed up in wonder up at the famous Coco de Mer that until then she had only ever read about.

'That's it,' Damiano confirmed, watching her rapt face through a rare shaft of sunlight cutting through the thick canopy of foliage above them. 'And that, *cara*,' he murmured from behind her, when she craned her neck to study the huge green husks suspended from the famous tree, 'is its fruit.' He slipped an arm around her slender waist, breathing in the light floral fragrance of her perfume as he whispered sexily against her ear, 'Renowned for its mystical sexual powers.'

He caught her tense little laugh as she glanced over her shoulder and met the wicked gleam in his eyes.

Whether they fought it or not, he thought, his senses

sharpened by the shrill sounds and earthy scents of the heated darkness, this thing between them was as untameable and as primitive as this forest.

'Is that because it's shaped like it is?' She giggled, her midriff rising and falling sharply against the warmth of his arm as she reminded him. They had chuckled over one of these "nuts" in the shop on the edge of the forest because, seeing it as they had with its husk removed—like two huge coconuts joined together—there had been no disputing that this rare and exotic seed was the exact shape and proportions of a woman's pelvis.

'It grows here and only here,' he answered her, with both arms coming around her now, 'which is why legend has it that this place is the original site of the Garden of Eden.'

'How can they know?' She laughed, her breathing tremulous, because he had bent his head to allow his teeth to graze the soft skin at the juncture of her neck and shoulder.

She was wearing a pure white diaphanous dress, virginal and flimsy, which was making his mind work overtime as he imagined her with nothing under it—nothing but the outline of her beautiful body—tantalising him, inviting him to rip it off and take her hard and spontaneously—as nature intended—here on the forest floor.

Voices coming through the trees splintered his overwrought imagination.

'Let's leave this place to the tourists,' he said huskily, releasing her.

They flew home with the sun streaking gold across the sea.

As Damiano drove them from the airfield the whole island was ablaze with the sunset. Flame-tipped trees touching the roadside burned amber as they climbed the forested hills, and a huge fruit bat, flying with a lazy movement of its long wings, made a dark silhouette against the fiery sky.

Ben was already in bed when they got back.

Tiptoeing into his room, Riva bent and kissed his sleepy

cheek. He stirred slightly as she stroked his hair, murmured softly, and then drifted back into a contented sleep.

'Buona notte, piccolo.'

A shaft of emotion pierced her as she saw Damiano do the same, that soft endearment sending such a gush of love for him washing over her that she was willing to do anything he wanted when he turned her towards him just outside Ben's door.

There was so much emotion in her eyes, Damiano noticed, but was it just for Benito? Was he fooling himself in thinking that a little of whatever was softening her lovely features and sending his defences into meltdown might possibly be for him?

When his lips brushed her cheek, and her face automatically tilted upwards to his, he felt his control being stretched to the limit in denying himself the pleasure of plundering that lovely mouth and then carrying her off to bed and keeping her there until she begged him to let her go. But his control won.

'Goodnight, Riva,' he murmured, breathing heavily as he dragged himself away.

Racked with frustration, Riva tossed and turned in bed. Damiano had taken her to paradise and back when he had made love to her that day in his bedroom and then literally—geographically—today, according to legend.

'The original site of the Garden of Eden', he'd called that forest, where the fruit of the coco de mer tree had mystical and sensual powers. But even that hadn't induced him to make love to her again, because when they had returned he had simply claimed work to do and had taken himself off to his study.

Turning over again onto her side, with her short strappy nightie riding up over her thighs, her gaze fell on the bedside cabinet and the small wooden replica of the 'seed' she had purchased to take back to England with her. Its provocative outline was clearly defined beneath the light of a rising moon.

Was it surprising, she thought, that it was believed to have the powers people claimed, when just seeing that sinful-looking seed made a woman so vibrantly aware of her own body?

She thought of Damiano, lying alone and most certainly naked in that massive bed. He was putting her through hell, and he knew it. They could have been together if it wasn't for her, their minds and bodies uniting, pleasuring each other; making love.

'Grab the passion,' Eloise had said. 'It is so beautiful while it lasts.'

She meant by marrying him, Riva realised, not sneaking off to his room in the middle of the night like a guilty mistress. But couples didn't marry nowadays because it was expected of them—simply the right thing to do. She couldn't—wouldn't!—put herself in the same position that Eloise Duval had found herself in. She wouldn't marry a man who didn't love her just because he'd decided it was his duty.

His room on the opposite side of the house was dimly lit. Only the external lights concealed amongst the shrubbery below windows that were flung open to the night showed the contours of his magnificent body—stretched out naked, as she had imagined, beneath the grey silk sheet he had pushed aside, leaving him exposed to the hip.

Dry-mouthed, heart racing, Riva hesitated in the doorway. Just a few short steps was all it would take to end this torture that she was putting them both through. But she had never instigated sex with a man before. Did she have the courage? All she had to do was drag back the sheet and climb in...

But then something brushed past her, a silent moth on velvet wings that had her hand coming up to brush at it with a startled cry.

The man in the bed moved, turning restlessly onto his back, but those few seconds were all it took, because like a mouse that had ventured too far into a lion's den suddenly

Riva lost her nerve, and before she had time to think she was pivoting away.

The beach as she came down onto it was bathed in moonlight, which was casting a bright silvery path across the restless sea.

Why was she afraid? she chided herself above the chirruping of crickets, wishing she had the courage to do what she knew would have come as second nature to most of the young women she mixed with. And the answer came back as though on the breeze that was teasing the loose ends of the short robe she had slipped on over her nightie: *because you love him so much you're just too terrified of getting hurt.*

And because of that she was out here alone, still aching for him now, knowing what it was like to be crushed beneath him in mindless passion, to feel the burning heat of his body as he lowered himself onto her, the thrill of his sliding into her, which made this hunger for him so much worse...

'Can anyone join in, or is this a private party?'

It was as though her desires had conjured him up out of the night.

'Wh-what are you doing here?' He too was wearing a robe—dark silk, knee-length. The gaping neck was exposing a good deal of very virile chest.

'I could ask the same thing of you.'

Quickly she uttered, 'I couldn't sleep.'

'Couldn't you?' His mouth twisted in a way that even in the shadows she could see was overtly sensual. 'I wonder why?'

'I was too hot.'

'Evidently. And I think not just because of the tropical humidity.'

Riva's breath caught in her lungs. 'Wh-what do you mean?' Did he know she had crept into his room? Had he been awake all along? Heard her muffled cry before she'd darted out of his room like a startled rabbit?

'Do you want me to spell it out?'

Her heart hammered against her ribs. 'I don't know what you're talking about,' she bluffed, dropping her gaze to his very masculine feet, thrust into leather-strapped sandals, spellbound in a world where even the moths conspired to betray her to him.

She ducked even as she thought it, as some night insect skimmed out of the shadows just over her head, attracted by the softly lit shrubbery above the beach.

'They won't hurt you, you know. These things probably fear you far more than you fear them.'

Riva pulled a wry face. 'That's what Mum always used to say.'

Although she wasn't looking at him she could sense his sympathetic smile. 'She sounds as though she was a very wise woman.'

'She was,' she responded. 'In most things. She was also a wonderful person, despite what you've always believed. Most of those things you were told—like that time she left the lodgings without paying—it wasn't like that at all. She was pretty, and men couldn't stop themselves from trying it on with her. That was what happened with that crumby landlord who owned the bedsit where we were living. He said he'd put up the rent to some extortionate rate and we'd have to get out if she didn't give in to what he was demanding of her. She refused to oblige and dragged me off out of there that night because he came on to her anyway. She was only trying to protect herself and me. She was dependable most of the time, but deep down she was so lonely and so insecure. That's why I was so happy when she found your uncle. She really loved him,' she stressed fervently, even though she knew it was like trying to convince a brick wall. 'They would have been happy together—I'm sure they would.'

The silence was impregnated only by the waves and the whistling of the lizards and the crickets and then, closer to hand, Damiano's heavily drawn breath. 'Don't you think I haven't realised that by now?'

Had he? The face upturned to his was scored with hurt and disbelief.

'Riva…'

As he touched her arm she flinched, her hands coming up, palms outwards. She couldn't deal with this now. 'No, don't say anything!'

She swung away from him, trekking down the beach, refusing to let him see the emotion that was falling as silent tears down her cheeks.

Without heed for anything else she was kicking off her sandals, pulling off her robe and then her nightdress, discarding them as she went, leaving them like a trail of shed skin behind her in the moonlight as she waded, naked, into the warm sea.

The elemental power and strength of the ocean invigorated and rejuvenated her, washing away her pain in the pounding surf.

When she turned towards the beach she heard Damiano coming purposefully towards her, his arms slicing powerfully through the dark water.

'Don't ever do that to me again! *Santo cielo!* I thought that you were going to—'

'Going to what? Try to swim back to England?' She laughed now, making out concern on his handsome, darkly shadowed face, knowing that that wasn't what he'd thought at all.

'It isn't anything to laugh about,' he reprimanded. 'These currents are dangerous. It was a very foolish thing to do, and if it wasn't considered so politically incorrect I think I'd turn you over my knee and spank you.'

'You'd have a job on.' She was giggling now because, like her, he was treading water, and because she was buoyant with a heady breathless excitement. Did his obvious concern for her mean that he *cared*? 'So what are you going to do to me instead?'

Why was she behaving like this? Like some provocative nymph hell-bent on her own destruction? Because it *would* be destruction—emotionally, at any rate, she warned herself. But at that moment she was riding too high to care.

'Do you really want to know?' His voice, losing some of its anger, was infused with sensual promise, and all the more exciting because she knew that whatever that promise was, it was about to be delivered.

As he lunged for her she let out a shriek, her excitement heightening as all her squealing and struggling to get away from him proved futile when he brought her with lifeguard strength and determination into shallower water.

Her feet touched down—but only just—and as she made a grab for him to stop herself going under, for the first time she realised with a frisson shooting through her that he was every bit as naked as she was.

'Get the general idea?' he crooned, as both her arms went around his neck, and in the moonlight she could see the satisfaction in his wickedly crooked grin.

Yes, she got the general idea, because with his hands supporting her buttocks her legs automatically went around him too, leaving her wide open to whatever he had in mind.

Between her splayed thighs she felt the tepid water bathe the entrance to her womb, a soft and soothing sensation, arousing in itself, because it showed her just how exposed and accessible she was to him.

With her cheek against his unshaven jaw, her hands glorying in the wet warmth of his powerful shoulders, she gave a deep guttural groan as the fluid in the yearning space between her legs was suddenly being displaced, giving way to his hard, hot, rampant penetration.

It was the most incredible sensation she had ever known. Never had she been so aware of her own body. Her proud nipples grazed by the rasping friction of that masculine chest, she flung her head back, inviting his mouth to taste and nip and suck, while those secret lips of her own contracted around him, drawing him in, accommodating his shaft as it sank more and more deeply inside of her.

She moaned softly against the flexing strength of his shoulder, tasting the salty wetness of his sun-bronzed skin.

She had loved him then and she loved him now, she acknowledged. Totally and unconditionally. Joined to him, with his body filling hers, the past and the future didn't seem to matter—only the present, these glorious moments stolen from eternity, where only pleasure and sublime happiness reigned.

Here in paradise they were just one man and one woman—like Adam with his Eve—where it was so easy to believe that everything was perfect, and everyday life and the things that could so easily come between them were far away.

Here, there was only sea and sound and sensation, the sound of the air rushing through their urgent lungs above the dark caressing ocean, and the sensation, as if she was part of it—in tune with its pounding rhythm—as Damiano started to move.

Thighs gripping his hard, warm flanks, she was moving with him, opening herself wide as he pushed harder and deeper, crying out because the pleasure was so unbearably intense. He was reaching some part of her, some secret inner chamber of her body that was suddenly sending her senses into free-fall, tipping her over the precipice of pleasure into an Eden of throbbing ecstasy.

With the contractions of her body still pulsing, she was aware of his own orgasm building, but a second before the moment of expulsion he uttered a groan from deep in his throat and pulled himself swiftly out of her.

She had been anticipating the spurt of his seed with almost delirious expectation, and instead he had allowed it to spill out into the surging ocean—become part of it—which made her feel ridiculously bereft.

Held close against his body, as their breathing returned to normal, she tried to wriggle out of his arms, but he wouldn't let her go.

'Marry me, Riva.' Those deeply uttered words, which sounded more like a command than a request, had her eyelids closing tight against the longing to accept.

He would be hers if she did. If she put herself out of her misery and agreed to share his life and the pleasures that being his wife would undoubtedly bring her—the most important one being a stable family life for Ben—but for how long?

He had said he had never lied to her, and he obviously wouldn't. Which was why he had never said he loved her, she thought achingly—because he didn't. If he did he wouldn't have pulled away from her just now in the way he had. But he clearly didn't really want to commit himself to her, or risk her getting pregnant again, despite his proposal of marriage. Why would he? She was just a nobody with a background anyone would have been dubious of, while he was rich and respected and influential and could have the pick of any woman he chose.

Whether or not he was sorry for what he had done in the past…and with that amazing and unexpected admission he'd made about Marcello and Chelsea earlier he'd come very close to it…nothing could alter that. She was still the daughter of a convicted fraudster whom he'd inadvertently made pregnant, and who was foolish enough to believe in marrying for love, while he came from a family where emotions were stifled and men and women did their duty, no matter what the cost. So how could she marry him, knowing that he'd only asked her because he felt he owed it to her, and that when this driving sexual desire he had for her wore off he would probably resent her? How could she possibly bear it? And how could that create a happy and stable upbringing for Ben?

'Please, Damiano…' Her face was ravaged by the conflict going on inside her as she tugged purposefully out of his arms.

She made short shrift of reaching the beach and, scrambling out of the water, started gathering up her clothes.

'"Please, Damiano", what?' He had been hot on her heels, and now an imperative hand was pulling her round to face him. His body ran with gleaming rivulets beneath the subtle lighting of the beach. 'What are you trying to tell me, Riva? I thought when you came to my room tonight that you had at last…'

'Had at last what?' She looked up at him, trying to make sense of his shadowy features. 'Come to my senses?' Tugging away from him, she started shrugging awkwardly into her robe.

'That isn't what I was going to say…' He came after her, impatiently snatching up his own robe as he did so. 'But you must admit that it is the most logical way forward.'

The most logical way forward? The coldness of that statement sent a shiver coursing through her.

'Why?' she demanded, hurting. 'So you can have your son with you all the time?'

'*Santo cielo!* Of course that isn't the only reason. I want him to have my name, *sì*. But I'm offering you my name also. And I do want him with me all the time. Is that so unreasonable?'

And what about me? The words choked her, because how could she have imagined that what they had just done could possibly mean anything other than just a pleasurable experience for him? OK, he wanted to give her his name, but only because—as she'd already come to realise, and as he'd made so plain from the way he had just said it—his sense of duty demanded it. That and the main fact that it was the only sure way of guaranteeing custody of his son.

'No,' she said, flatly, refusing to enter into a one-sided marriage even if he or Eloise Duval or even the Man in the Moon tried to persuade her she should.

'And that's your final answer?'

'That's my final answer,' she asserted, and, clutching her nightdress and sandals to her breast, broke into a run to get away from him before he could try and change her mind.

Which he could so easily have done, she realised with her heart breaking, because she knew from the finality of his tone as he'd asked that question that he wouldn't ask her again.

CHAPTER ELEVEN

'So...apart from looking stupendously tanned,' Olivia Redwood commented when Riva walked into her office in grey leggings and a white sleeveless belted tunic that unintentionally showed off her sun-kissed skin, 'how did it go?'

Riva shrugged, tried to sound nonchalant. 'OK.'

From beneath heavily shadowed eyes the woman viewed her sceptically. 'Only OK?'

Those eyes were too probing, but, reminding herself that her boss didn't need to know about Damiano, with another dismissive little shrug, Riva said, 'We sorted out what needed to be sorted out.'

Only they hadn't. They hadn't been able to agree a suitable arrangement for Ben. Damiano wanted joint custody and she still hadn't yet agreed to it. How could she, when she couldn't guarantee that he wouldn't try to take him away from her if she did? She couldn't forget how grim-faced he had looked as he'd driven them home from the airport two days ago, his stunning features shuttered to everything but Ben's sobbed little appeal, as his father was leaving the flat, as to *why* his dad had to go. When Damiano had gently disentangled the little arms from around his neck and promised, in a remarkably choked voice, that he'd come back soon, it had all but ripped the heart out of Riva.

After he had gone she'd felt dejected and alone and, like Ben, who was wandering around the flat like a lost little soul, she was missing Damiano so much that she'd started questioning herself as to whether or not she hadn't made a mistake in not agreeing to marry him. Not for her own sake, but at least for Ben's, she argued with herself, trying nevertheless to blot out the warmth of the man's charismatic smile, the rich, deep timbre of his voice, and the feel of those slightly callused hands on her body.

'And does that "sorting out" in any way include the sound of wedding bells?' It was an invitation from Olivia to share some domestic dialogue—rare for the woman who had built Redwood Interiors single-handed, Riva thought, wondering what had sparked this sudden interest in her private life.

'Definitely not,' she responded, and was glad when her boss took the hint and didn't pursue the subject any further.

Over the next two or three weeks she was free from the turmoil of seeing Damiano again, since he'd been called away on some business in Europe. His regular calls to Ben, however, had her heart leaping every time he came on the phone, even though the warmth with which she heard him greet his son was sadly lacking from his voice whenever Ben handed her back the handset.

'So, how have you been, Riva?' Tonight he lingered to talk—and not just about Ben. 'No unusual fatigue?' he enquired smoothly when she told him rather abruptly that she was fine. 'No sickness? No missed period?'

She knew he must have heard the way she sucked in her breath. 'You took care of that, remember?' Swiftly she turned her back on Ben who had run over to switch on the television. If Damiano hadn't taken care of it, how easy it would have been to have found herself in the same position again, swept away by her love for him and the ecstasy of one crazily abandoned moment!

'Sì, I did. But it's not the safest method in the world. Apart from which, you kept Benito's existence from me. How do I know you wouldn't try to do it with a second child?'

'For heaven's sake!' She moved out into the hall, aware of

Ben's little ears pricking up at the sharpness of her tone. 'I said I'm fine. Why won't you believe me?' It was almost as though he wanted her to be pregnant! she thought hysterically.

Suddenly it hit her that, in spite of the way he'd withdrawn from her so swiftly when they had been making love in the sea that night, he might now probably be thinking that if he *had* made her pregnant she would in all probability have considered marrying him. After all, he knew the difficulties she had faced in raising one child single-handedly, without the added responsibility of coping with another tiny baby as well. Of course he would imagine that she would automatically turn to him in that case, which in turn would mean that he wouldn't have to suffer this role of absentee father that he clearly hated. Then he could have his son—and however many more babies he cared to implant in her willing womb—under his roof, where he wanted them. Permanently. As well as a warm and willing bed-partner until such time as his need of her wore off and he reached his boredom threshold with his very unsuitable wife.

'Tough luck, Damiano,' she exhaled bitterly, and cut him off before the tremor in her voice gave her away.

She was glad he was away, and yet over the days that followed she missed him like crazy. It didn't help at all witnessing how much Ben missed him too.

'When's Daddy coming?' he kept asking, with heart-rending poignancy.

'As soon as he's back in the UK, poppet,' she assured him, picking him up. He was getting to be quite a weight for her slight frame. Like his father, she thought, he promised to be a fine strong man when he grew up, and despite his reddish-brown hair and his impish little smile he was getting to look more like Damiano every day. 'He'll always be there for you, Benito.' Of that, at least, she could be certain. 'It's just that he's got a very important job to do at the moment, but he's coming to see you the moment he gets back.'

During the day she tried losing herself in her work—which

might have helped, she thought, if she hadn't kept seeing Damiano's face in every stranger she passed on the street, or hearing his voice as it was when he was making love to her: husky, unbelievably arousing, raw-edged with the depth of his desire.

It didn't help to make her feel any better either when, on picking Ben up from his childminder one evening, Kate Shepherd told her, 'He's getting on fine, but he does tend to get a bit distracted.' Fondly she ruffled Ben's hair, which was getting enviably thick—like Damiano's. 'All he wants to do these days is talk about his dad!'

I know how he feels, Riva thought achingly, wishing life wasn't so complicated. If she could have met Damiano in other circumstances he might have fallen in love with her despite her background, wanted her to marry him because...

She stamped down on that runaway thought before it could even take shape. She hadn't, and he hadn't. In fact if it wasn't for him trying to trip her up by seducing her out of his moral duty to protect his uncle's interests five years ago he would never even have looked her way, let alone fallen in love with her!

That, though, still didn't stop her thinking about him and regretting that she wasn't as brave as Eloise—to 'grab the passion', as that elegant lady had put it, and then live on her memories of that passion for the rest of her life. Because wasn't that what she was doing anyway? she contemplated, wondering if she would ever find a man who could make her feel quite the same way as Damiano had—and not just physically, but in every other sense as well. Maybe she would, she thought, without too much conviction. One day.

And one day, when Ben was a little older she would start dating seriously, she decided, because that was the only way to meet a man that she wanted to settle down with, wasn't it? For now, though, it was enough for her just to come home in the evenings and carry on with her design studies, indulge in some childlike games with Ben, and play a little game with herself in seeing how long she could go without thinking about Damiano as she tried to concentrate on reading Ben his bedtime story. It was enough too—when she finally got him off to sleep and she'd finished her studies for the evening—to play the CD she'd bought since coming back from the Seychelles of that French singer Eloise liked so much. It was all too easy then to convince herself that it was because she liked the songs so much that she left it on Replay, rather than because of the memories it conjured up as she worked away at her cross-stitch, which she was pleased to see was nearly completed.

One morning, going into Olivia's office to return a brochure, she overheard her boss mentioning Damiano and the Old Coach House to someone over the phone.

With her office door open, and her chair swivelled towards the window, Olivia had her back to Riva and hadn't heard her walk in. And, though Riva didn't make a habit of listening to other's people's telephone conversations, the information she picked up in those few moments made her want to turn and run.

Except that her feet wouldn't seem to move before Olivia swivelled round on her chair and noticed her standing there.

'Riva…' The woman looked awkward—uncomfortable—as, her call over with, the phone clattered back on its rest. 'I didn't realise you'd come in.'

That much was obvious, Riva thought, hurting, but managed to say calmly, 'So he's gone with another designer? Is that it?'

Olivia's power-dressed shoulders lifted almost indiscernibly. 'That's how it goes in this business, Riva. I thought you might already have known…'

Too numb to speak, Riva shook her head.

'Oh, well…' Olivia smiled, treating it lightly. 'There'll be plenty more projects in the future. In the meantime, there's no reason at all to be upset.'

Upset!

The agonising cry that screamed through her brain was like that of a tortured animal. Nevertheless, she gave an apparently careless little shrug. 'You win some—you lose some.' She even tried for a smile, but she could feel her lips wobbling under the weight of her distress.

So he had just been indulging her even in that! Playing with her as he had always done, gaining her trust and then slamming it right back in her face the instant he was tired of whatever game he was playing. Well, she'd known that, hadn't she? she thought, harrowed. She just hadn't realised that he would do it in such a demoralising and humiliating way. And if Olivia had chosen not to tell her that her ideas had been sidestepped for someone else's until she'd discovered it for herself—well, that was her prerogative. She was the boss, after all. She could run Redwoods in any way she chose.

Hurt more than she could express by Damiano's under-hand actions, Riva decided not to give him the satisfaction of letting him know it. Consequently, when he rang that evening just after she had tucked Ben up for the night, she made up her mind not even to mention it for the time being.

'Ben's asleep,' she told him casually, wondering why he had left it so late to call.

'I guessed he might be.' His deep tones washed over her, dark and oh, so treacherously caressing. 'It's you I wanted to speak to.'

'Oh?' What did he want to speak to her about? she wondered torturously. Was he going to tell her what she had discovered by accident today? Apologise for not having the guts to tell her himself?

'It concerns Eloise.'

'Why? What's wrong?' Anxiety filled her. 'She's all right, isn't she?'

There was a brief pause while she dreaded the worst. 'She's fine.'

'What, then?' Her caginess couldn't hide the bone-weakening relief in her voice.

'As you're probably aware, it's her birthday next week, and Françoise and André are flying over to England with her later this week. I'll be flying back to the UK myself at the weekend, and she's asked me to arrange a party for her at the Old Coach House on Monday. It'll be just a few of her friends and mutual acquaintances—but I'd like you and Ben to be there.'

She wanted to refuse. To stay as far away from Damiano as she could—which was the only way she would ever get over him, she realised—but she couldn't. He was Ben's father, and that made Eloise Ben's great-grandmother. Besides, Riva was very fond of the old lady, and it was her birthday.

'There's just one thing...'

Riva tensed, catching something in the silky quality of his voice that put all her instincts on high alert.

'I've organised caterers and florists to arrive during the afternoon, and as Eloise will be at the hairdresser's someone will need to make sure that everything is done exactly as it should be. Could you be there to oversee things for me?'

'How can I?' Riva's head swam as she wondered why he had even imagined she would be able to take time off when she had only just come back from being away for a month—at his insistence—already. 'It's a working day!'

'All I'm asking is a couple of hours,' he stated, with infuriating disregard for putting her career in further jeopardy. 'Monday, then,' he established, leaving no room for argument as he rang off.

Surprisingly, Olivia Redwood didn't turn a hair when Riva very gingerly requested a couple of hours away from the office the following Monday.

'Take the whole afternoon,' the woman responded, remarkably generously—far more generously than Riva could have dared to hope.

Arranging to pick Ben up from pre-school after she had finished at the Old Coach House, Riva turned along the estate road and pulled up outside. She hadn't been there for weeks, and it was with a piercing stab to her heart that she remembered how enthusiastically she had tripped up those steps on that first day.

The ancient board advertising the big house had a huge '*SOLD*' sign emblazoned across it. So someone had bought it at last, she thought distractedly, guessing that only a developer would want it, to turn into money-spinning luxury apartments or—worse—to pull it down and erect some unsightly modern building in its place.

Deciding there was nothing she could do about it, even if she'd wanted to, although years ago it would have been something she might well have protested over, she did, however, feel a twinge of anxiety as to what any adverse development so close to the Old Coach House might mean for Eloise. Damiano's grandmother obviously liked peace and country views. She hoped this sale wouldn't mean her being deprived of them as she used the spare key she still had on her key-ring to let herself into the house.

There was an air of serenity about the place—so different from the tight, tense atmosphere generated when she had been there with Damiano, fighting her hopeless lack of resistance to him as she'd battled to keep him from finding out about Ben.

Tripping lightly upstairs to the main sitting room, to wait for the caterers and the florists, she came to a shocked standstill in the doorway.

Glasses gleamed on the damask cloth gracing the table that was to be used for the evening's buffet, alongside cutlery wrapped in crisp white napkins and sparkling china. Pink roses in a reservoir in the centre were spectacularly displayed, while in strategic places around the room other bowls of professionally arranged flowers added brightness and colour and sweet scents such as she would have appreciated if she hadn't been so winded by the sight of them.

Everything had been done. How could it have been? she

wondered, totally bewildered. What was Damiano playing at? No one was supposed to have been coming until three!

Then she heard the front door close in the hall below and swung round, her head spinning. Had she left it open? She hadn't heard anyone drive in, so who…?

'I can feel the vibes now,' Damiano's voice assured her from the top of the stairs, 'so don't say anything, Riva.'

In a dark suit that showed off the sleek, powerful lines of his body, and a white shirt that accentuated his olive skin and the dark hair curling so tantalisingly against his collar, she had always thought he looked his most sensational. Yet beneath the glow of his healthy tan he looked unusually strained.

'Don't say anything?' Unconsciously she slumped against the doorframe, the sight of his hard, executive image making her weak at the knees. 'You force me to take more time off. Bring me here under false pretences—again! What the hell do you think you're playing at, Damiano? What gives you the right to think you can control other people's lives?'

He threw out his hands, remarkably unperturbed by her outburst. 'You only ever seem to want to speak to me these days unless it's on Ben's behalf. How else could I even hope to get you on your own?'

Now his reasons for bringing her here became all too clear. She had rejected his proposal and quite obviously he had decided not to press her again. Perhaps he was even relieved, she considered agonisingly, to realise that he had been mercifully released from his so-called duty to her. Yet he knew from the way she always responded to him that she had no defence against this dangerous attraction that always manifested itself when they were alone together. She could feel it now, licking along her veins and causing her breath to move shallowly through her lungs, just from the way his gaze was tugging over her simple white V-necked top and tight black skirt.

'Well, since I'm wasting valuable time away from the office, you won't mind if I don't appreciate being brought here on a fool's errand,' she returned, her breathing erratic as she made to get out of there and away from him as fast as she could.

And she might have succeeded if his arms hadn't come up to effectively block the doorway, so that she had to draw herself up swiftly to avoid colliding with him.

'Let me out of here, Damiano.' She had intended it to sound like a warning. Instead it came out sounding like a desperate appeal.

'Why so panicky?' He lifted his hands from the doorframe, turning them over in a gesture of feigned innocence. 'What can you possibly be afraid of—other than yourself?'

And that was the truth of it, she thought, despairing with herself. Because even now, when every instinct of self-survival was leaping to defend her from the danger he presented, her treacherous femininity was urging her to strain towards him, to feel the texture of that immaculate suit under her hands as she slid her arms around his neck and forced his lips down to hers, as she drank in the heady potion of his kiss and her body acknowledged the hardening strength of his.

'Don't be silly,' she breathed rather inanely, because her mouth felt dry and her heart was fluttering like a large Seychelles moth in her chest.

'Then why are you so nervous?'

'I'm not.'

A sceptical eyebrow lifted. 'No? The trembling mouth, that panicky look in those beautiful eyes.' He was moving closer, and now she could smell his cologne, sense the predatory instinct in him like a large cat stalking its prey. 'It's very becoming, but not quite the response I expected of a woman who refused a wedding ring and yet was quite happy to become my mistress.'

'I've never said I'd be your mistress.'

That doubting eyebrow climbed higher. 'That wasn't quite the impression you gave me when we were away.'

Because I never stopped loving you! her heart screamed,

while she struggled to appear calm and collected in light of all he was saying. *And because, deep down, I thought I could make you love me,* her brain tagged on, ridiculing her now for being such a stupid, stupid fool.

'The fact is that we never have been able to slake this ridiculous craving for each other, have we, *cara*? Time couldn't kill it. Self-denial certainly couldn't. In fact abstinence only increased the need—like a pressure cooker without any means of letting the steam escape. Perhaps the only way to turn off the pressure is to let it run its course. Perhaps that's the only way either of us will be able to view the other objectively—as we have to for Ben's sake—without this impossible crazy inferno always flaring up whenever our paths have to cross.'

Ridiculous. Impossible. Crazy. Every syllable he uttered was like a nail being driven into her heart. If he couldn't repay the debt he felt he owed her by marrying her, he would have her anyway, until he had purged himself of this 'ridiculous'—as he called it—addiction she held for him, which he clearly resented.

Every straining cell in her body was urging her to accept his proposition, because the promise of that degree of rapture with him—for however short a time—and then being able to walk away when it had run its course—as he was so convinced it would—was almost too much to resist. But she couldn't accept—because it wouldn't burn itself out. Not for her, at any rate. And at the end of it he would be the one to walk away unscathed, while she would only have delayed the inevitable and unbearable pain she knew would unquestionably follow.

'I won't be your mistress,' she stated flatly, feeling like a starving woman who was passing up the last life-sustaining meal she would ever have.

'No?' He gave her a sort of resigned half-smile, but then he shrugged and said, 'Pity. But then it's probably for the best. We wouldn't want to give our son false hope, would we?'

How could he treat it so lightly, when her heart was bleeding from his indifference to her feelings and his obvious lack of feeling for her?

'Is that all you have to say? Because if it is I'm sure you won't mind if I get back to work and make up the precious time I've wasted in coming here.' Hot colour blazed along her cheekbones and her voice was trembling from the emotion she was trying to hold back. 'You want everything your own way, Damiano—and you just use people to get it. You always did—no matter who got hurt. Well, you can't hurt me any more.' Like hell he couldn't! she thought, wanting only to get out of there before she broke down completely. 'And you're certainly never, ever going to use me again. I'll be here tonight—with Ben—but only because it's for Eloise. Now, if you don't mind, I've more important things to do than stand here engaging in a pointless conversation with you!'

She finished on a sob, fleeing out through the door before he could realise how much his imperviousness was torturing her.

'Just one last thing...'

That lazy drawl behind her stopped her as she reached the top of the stairs.

Crazily expectant, heart thumping, she half turned to face him, the tears she was fighting to control already glistening in her eyes.

'You left something behind when you were here last. Some samples, I think you call them. They're still where you left them,' he said, his strained-looking features impassive—like a stranger, or an employer who was telling her he no longer needed her services. 'Perhaps you'd like to pick them up on your way out.'

Turning away from him, she tore blindly down the stairs. What had she been expecting? she demanded of herself. A change of heart? What else could he have offered her when he couldn't give her the one thing she wanted most—his love?

She was crying freely, her tears unimpeded now he could no longer see her, as she stumbled along to his grandmother's private sanctuary at the other end of the house. She and Damiano were a lost cause, she thought agonisingly. Like the ones she had fought so loyally with Chelsea, even when she'd known that in the end it would all be hopeless. They never had been an item, she reminded herself fiercely, and she must accept that—no matter how much it hurt.

Turning sightlessly into the room she had created her plans for all those weeks before, focusing on her samples on the table, quickly she scooped them up, remembering how earnestly she had worked—and how gullibly—how...

Brushing tears from her eyes, she blinked several times, unable to believe what she was seeing. *He hadn't... He couldn't have. But he had!*

CHAPTER TWELVE

DROPPING her pad of samples back down on the table, trying to bring focus into her dazed mind, she turned her head this way and that, studying every aspect of the light and airy space, unable to take it in, pivoting round and round.

It was the finished version of all that she had planned for this room. Her nostrils came alive now to the smell of fresh paint, new flooring and fabrics. Right down to the smallest detail. Her Greek theme, which encompassed everything that was serene and beautiful and timeless, he had used to the full—from the touches of marble, soft colours and the unobtrusive lighting, to the tasteful and classically themed paintings he had had selected for the walls.

Beyond the patio doors the marble figure she had only envisaged graced the centre of the new mosaic-tiled terrace, and a silver ribbon of water cascaded through delicately sculpted hands into a natural pool.

He must have had people working round the clock to get it finished in time for Eloise's birthday, she realised, staggered, but he had had *her*, Riva's, plans and designs carried out to the letter. He'd even included things she had talked to him about while they had been away, when she hadn't even realised he had been pumping her. Just the way he had five years ago—except that he had used that shrewd intelligence to honour her skills and to please her this time, rather than to bring about her downfall.

'Well?' he prompted, so that she swung round, saw him standing there in the doorway. 'What do you think?'

Tall and dark and commanding, he appeared so calm, he might have been asking her what she thought about the weather.

She just stood there, open-mouthed, shaking her head, too overwhelmed to speak.

'I—I don't understand...' Somehow she found her voice, looking around her in awe of how much he had accomplished in so short a time—which meant he must have been liaising with the studio the whole time they had been in the Seychelles! 'When did you arrange all this?'

'At the same time as I arranged with Olivia to grant you extended leave—that day after I'd met you and Benito in the park.'

'You mean you'd already organised it with her?' She exhaled, realising that her boss had known she'd be taking time off even before Riva had asked her. And suddenly a few other things became strikingly clear. Like why Olivia had been so keen to know how Riva's holiday with Ben's father had gone—because she would obviously have realised it was Damiano—and why the woman had looked so pleased with herself when she'd given her time off to come here this afternoon—because she'd known all about this all along and yet, loyal to her illustrious client, she hadn't breathed a word! 'But I thought you weren't interested in my plans? That there wasn't even going to be a job...' Her voice tailed away as she struggled to remember exactly how things had been left. 'You let me believe you'd given it to someone else.'

'You let yourself believe that,' he said, his mouth pulling to one side. 'As for the rest—you managed to convince yourself of that too. As you were always so ready to think the worst about me, I didn't see any point in denying it—although I'm not blaming you for that. I'm well aware that respect has to be earned, and that I threw away whatever respect you might have had for me a long time ago.'

What was he saying? Head cocked to one side, she searched his dark inscrutable features, a groove of pained bewilderment between her brows.

'Well...?' He was looking over her head at the result of all her hard planning. And perhaps he felt robbed of his Italian pride in admitting what he had just admitted, she thought, because he merely shrugged and said on a strangely laboured breath, 'Is it to your expectations?'

Emotion welled up inside her. She still couldn't believe that he had valued her ideas enough to follow them all through—and so quickly. It was a lovely surprise for his grandmother, and an even bigger one for her, but it was what he had just said about her losing respect for him that was making her head whirl with so many hopes.

'It more than exceeds them,' she whispered, equally as breathless as he'd seemed a moment ago. 'There's only one thing...' She was looking critically up at the large landscape hanging on the principal wall.

'What?' he prompted, frowning.

'That doesn't belong there,' she remarked assuredly. Already she was heading for the door. 'Could you take it down?'

When she returned she was carrying a very large flat package, wrapped in plain brown paper. It was, Damiano thought, almost too big for her to manage on her own.

'Here. Let me.' He took it from her while she tore at the wrapping, unable to take his eyes off her. She was small and seductive and so utterly, utterly desirable. He wanted to toss this painting—or whatever it was—aside, and just take her in his arms and make love to her. But if he so much as made a wrong move it would only drive her away, and he couldn't let that happen, however hard it was to keep the almost uncontrollable urge in check.

Now, at her request, he hung the large framed picture onto the hook where the landscape had been hanging. He felt the air being sucked out of his lungs as he stood back to look at it.

It was a hand-stitched tableau depicting a Grecian woman in flowing robes reclining before her weaving loom. In the less distinct background an ancient battle raged. The colours in the foreground were vibrant—the subject was a study in longing and repressed emotion. It was someone's labour of love, which had obviously cost many painstaking hours to create.

'The mythical Greek goddess Penelope.' He moved so that the picture was in the centre of his field of vision. 'You said you wanted something dramatic for this wall...' His breathing came deeply from the impact it had made upon him. 'But this is...phenomenal.'

'Thank you.'

The almost shy way in which she said it pulled his gaze away from the tableau. His eyes rested on her face with a dark, almost pained intensity.

'It's yours, isn't it?' His voice seemed to crack as he asked it. 'This is what you were working on so diligently while we were away. And also that evening when I found out about Benito, though I was too angry that night to take much in...' His attention turned to the picture again, and he stepped back to take the whole thing in. 'The goddess Penelope, who weaved all day and every night unpicked what she had done to appear constantly busy to her would-be suitors, simply to remain faithful to her husband for all the years he was away at war.'

'It belongs to Eloise,' Riva told him resolutely. 'She stayed true to your grandfather, even though he broke her heart because he couldn't love her back in the way she loved him.'

'And you give her this?' Waving a hand towards the wall, he was looking at Riva, studying her small and beautiful features, her mesmerising eyes, her petite upturned nose and the sensuous mouth that was set with the familiar determination he knew so well. He couldn't get over how generous she was.

How caring. And to his grandmother as well as his son. 'It's perfect for this room. But it looks like a lifetime's work. How long did it take you?'

'Four—' she gave a dismissive little shrug '—four and a half years.'

'And is it this that kept the suitors from *your* door, *carissima*? Or was it your subconscious desires that kept you faithful to me?'

With her hand coming up, every instinct of self-preservation had her backing away from him. 'Don't…'

'Answer me.' The command seemed almost torn from his throat. 'I need to know.'

'Why?' Her love for him was an unbearable ache in her chest. She couldn't trust him. How could she, even if he had done all this? Unconsciously her gaze lifted to the newly refurbished room. Even if he had said something he hadn't followed up just now—before she'd gone out to her car— about her losing respect for him. 'Why do you need to know? Why? When I know deep down you probably still think you were right about Mum and me not being good enough for your family—even if you let me think you'd changed your mind about her that night on the beach? When I know you still look down on me, and that I'll never be good enough for you—even if you do rate me as a designer?' she tagged on with heart-rending poignancy. 'I know you wouldn't even have looked my way in the beginning if you hadn't wanted to protect Marcello—or now if it weren't for Ben.'

'*Santo cielo!*' His hands were held outwards as he came towards her, shaking his head in a sort of bewildered disbelief. 'What more would you have me do? Haven't I made up for the things you're accusing me of? Shown you by the very nature of my feeling for you that I'll regret what I did for the rest of my days? But if my punishment is to be cast adrift and suffer eternal hell without you, *cara*, then I'll have to take it as my just deserts for hurting you.' His strong face was ravaged by an emotion so tangible she felt she was drowning in the depths of his pain. 'Know only that I love you, *carissima*, and that I'm eternally sorry for what I did to Chelsea. I can't make it up to her—or Marcello—but if you'll just give me the chance all I want to do is spend the rest of my life making her daughter happy.'

She couldn't believe he was saying this. That he was actually laying all his cards on the table with such soul-baring contrition.

'And as for you not being good enough for me, *amore*, you're twice the person I'll ever be. You're loving and generous and amusing, and my heart wanted you even when my head was being too stubborn and pompous to admit it. When you were innocent and naïve and running around outside, cutting your feet like a little waif because you didn't have the sense to keep your shoes on.' His smile indulged her as his hand cupped her face, warm and tender and strong. 'And I took that away from you.' He was stroking her hair, his voice self-denigrating, and the arm circling her waist was meeting no resistance now. 'Even though you were pretending to be like all the other women I always managed to get myself involved with—sophisticated, without a thought in their heads other than which dinner party they would be attending next, or whether they were wearing the right clothes and make-up to be seen in public—you weren't like them at all. And I was experienced enough to have known better—I should have realised.'

'Maybe I was just too good an actress,' she murmured regretfully, ashamed of the part she had played with him five years ago, the web of deception she'd woven around herself to try and win his love.

'Maybe.' He laughed softly, running a finger down the curve of her jaw, taking in her softly tousled hair, the striking flecks in her beautiful green eyes, that oh, so kissable mouth, as though he had never really looked at her before. 'I'm glad you were—otherwise we probably wouldn't have our son, would we?'

'You really mean that? You're actually glad that it happened?'

His dark eyes were incredulous. 'Are you kidding? More than you'll ever know. I love you, *carissima*. Why do you think I kept asking you to marry me?'

She couldn't think straight. The only thing spinning round and round in her head was that this wonderful man she loved actually loved *her*!

'But I thought—'

'You thought what?'

'That you only wanted to marry me because of Ben. That you—'

'It seems you've spent too much time thinking instead of looking. Why do you think I went to the lengths I did to get you here in the first place? OK, perhaps I didn't realise then how much you meant to me, that this feeling I had for you was more than just desire. You had found your way under my skin far more deeply than I wanted to admit, and I wanted you. But I wanted to make you pay for my wanting you, and only found myself getting in deeper and deeper. I was insanely jealous when I thought you were in a relationship with someone else. When I discovered that you had a son—and that he was mine…'

He was shaking his head, the loss he felt because of the years he'd missed out of Ben's little life sending shafts of love and guilt through Riva in equal measure.

'I wanted you to know. Believe me I did,' she stressed, regretting every minute that she had kept the two of them apart. 'And I especially didn't want to deprive my little boy of his father.'

'Then why didn't you come to me?' he breathed, his anguish palpable. 'Oh, I know what I said, but you surely must have realised that I wouldn't have turned you away?'

'How could I know?' she murmured sadly. 'I'd given my heart to you, but you were so cold and so superior that I could only guess at how you would have reacted if I'd written and told you I was pregnant—especially after what you said about it all being a plan to trap you.' The groan that came from deep within him expressed total disgust with himself. 'On top of that, I hadn't exactly been too forthcoming with the truth.'

'The way I was in those days, I can understand why.' He exhaled heavily. 'You had it tough, and the least I could have done was try to understand. But to keep something so precious as your virginity from me…and then to sacrifice it to a man who didn't show you the consideration he would certainly have shown if he'd known…' His breath shuddered through him from the depth of his remorse. 'You should have told me,' he concluded deeply.

'That I'd never slept with anyone before? That you were the first man I'd ever wanted in that way? You were so experienced and so scary, and I was so in love with you, I was afraid you'd dump me if you found out how green I really was. After we…did it…' even now she still felt absurdly embarrassed talking about it with him '…I couldn't bear you looking at me so angrily, as though I was stupid and thoroughly irresponsible. I know I was, but it hurt so much knowing you thought it. That's why I pretended to be on the pill.'

He caught her tenderly to him. 'Oh, *carissima*.' It was an agonised groan into the wildfire of her hair. 'I have a lot to make up for, and I want to start doing it as of now. I won't put any pressure on you to do anything you don't want to do, but do you think that one day you could find it in your heart to forgive me? To accept me as I am now and try to love me again as you did before? Or is that expecting too much of you, *amore*? If you say it is, then it will be no more than I deserve.'

His words triggered the memory of Eloise asking her if she was still punishing him. And she realised that subconsciously she had been—that one of the reasons for not giving herself to him so completely—as she so dearly longed to do—was because she felt she'd be betraying Chelsea. And yet in not doing so she'd been punishing herself as well.

'I do still love you,' she whispered, standing on tiptoe to draw his dark head down to her. 'Even when I thought I hated you, I think something inside me never actually stopped.'

His mouth moved tenderly over hers, and then more insistently as her lips parted beneath his in an urgent and mutually demanding kiss. For the first time, she thought, she was offering herself to him as an equal, as a loving partner, and her heart seemed to take flight as he pressed her closer to him while their bodies moved sinuously against each other's for the ultimate fulfilment their love demanded.

It seemed like an age before Damiano reluctantly forced himself to break off their kiss.

'As much as I'd like to make love to you—here and now— Eloise will be back at any moment. But I promise you, the instant the party's over it's going to be a long time before I let you out of my bed again. Your flat's rather small, so I'm afraid, *carissima*, that until you can get your design skills working again on every room in a boarded-up mansion, it will have to be my apartment in town.'

Riva frowned, searching his face until, seeing the amused satisfaction curling his lips, she darted a glance towards the patio doors.

Through the thick summer foliage she could just make out the old house, standing quietly serene in the afternoon sunlight.

'*You* bought it?' She didn't know whether to laugh or cry. She didn't think she could take any more wonderful surprises in one day!

'I put an offer in for the place weeks ago, and it was accepted. In fact I drove up there earlier to meet the agent with the keys.' He grinned, clearly pleased with himself, 'And walked down here as soon as I saw you drive in.'

That accounted for why she hadn't seen his car outside, Riva realised.

'That's one of the reasons I've been in Europe for three weeks—to organise the sale of Marcello's villa, as well as a couple of properties of my own. We're still keeping the Seychelles house—in fact you might like to consider it for our honeymoon,' he interjected dryly, 'but we need a clean start, and I want to settle here in England, with Eloise just down the drive, where she can still keep her independence but I can keep an eye on her. And because the other two most special people I know are here. Well?' he pressed, when she was too overwhelmed with joy and amazement at all he was saying to respond. 'What do you think?'

Now she laughed up at him, her emerald eyes dancing with that impishness he loved. 'About marrying you or about living there?'

He tapped her lovingly on the nose. 'Both,' he answered with a chuckle, still hardly daring to hope. 'What is it, *cara*?' Lines corrugated his forehead as he noticed the sudden clouding of her eyes.

'You won't get bored with me?' she put to him, rather tentatively.

'Bored with you?' His soft laughter was incredulous. 'Why on earth do you ask that?'

'You don't exactly have a good track record for your staying power in relationships,' she reminded him, almost sheepishly.

'Ah, I see,' he breathed, aware that she was referring in particular to the Magenta Boweringham article—and that disgruntled lady's public attempt to discredit him. 'I couldn't do the dishonest thing and pretend to feel something I didn't feel,' he explained simply. 'Because I'd never met the woman I wanted to marry. Until now...'

His voice held so much sincerity that it shook her to think she could ever have doubted him. Now, in answer to his questions about living at the manor and especially about marrying him, she murmured, 'I think they're both wonderful ideas,' adding teasingly, 'What took you so long to ask?'

'You'll pay for that—later,' he pledged, with an exciting promise in his eyes. But then on a more serious note, holding back from her a little, he asked, 'What about Benito? Do you think he'll be pleased that his *mamma* and *papà* have finally decided to do the decent thing?'

'Are you kidding?' She couldn't credit that he needed to ask. 'He thinks you're the best thing since sliced bread!' She laughed, to alleviate any concerns he might still be harbouring.

He gave a long, relieved sigh, drawing her back into his arms. 'I love you, *amore*,' he murmured deeply, and the way his powerful body trembled against hers only confirmed it.

'I love you too,' she whispered, unable to believe her heart could hold so much joy.

At first neither noticed the silent, elegant figure standing unobtrusively in the doorway. But turning her head, snuggling against Damiano's shoulder, Riva opened her eyes and spotted Eloise.

She was looking towards the main wall, and the tableau that Riva and Damiano had hung there. Those glittering eyes registered shock, amazement and then pure joy as her gaze dropped and met Riva's smile.

Love him, ma chère. *Grab the passion.* As her grandmother-in-law-to-be turned discreetly away, Riva could still hear those deeply accented words in her head—and something else that she read in the woman's discerning smile, which she already knew in her own heart.

She had it all.

It was something to be nurtured and treasured, she realised, looking up at this wonderful man who was offering her a lifetime of loving, and she knew without a shadow of doubt that this special love they shared was going to last for ever. And as she rested her head against his shoulder again, and her gaze strayed towards the tableau that they had hung together, that legendary lady of faithfulness seemed to be looking down on them both, and Riva almost imagined that she smiled.

PASSION AND THE PRINCE
by Penny Jordan

Prince Marco di Lucchesi can't hide his haughty disdain for Lily Wrightington—or his violent attraction to her! Can he trust himself to offer the protection she seeks *without* unleashing his passion?

ALESSANDRO'S PRIZE
by Helen Bianchin

Determined to get on with her newly single life, a break in Milan sounds ideal to Lily Parisi. Until she bumps into Alessandro del Marco, an enigmatic face from her past, and her plans come completely undone…

WIFE IN THE SHADOWS
by Sara Craven

In society's spotlight, Count Angelo Manzini bestows dutiful kisses on his apparently biddable new bride, Elena. But behind closed doors, Angelo is captivated by his countess's defiance…

AN INCONVENIENT OBSESSION
by Natasha Tate

Ethan Hardesty has it all…apart from Cate Carrington—the girl he loved and lost. But now the Carrington family's island is up for auction, providing him with the perfect opportunity to take her into the bargain!

On sale from 20th May 2011
Don't miss out!

*Available at WHSmith, Tesco, ASDA, Eason
and all good bookshops*
www.millsandboon.co.uk

FOR DUTY'S SAKE
by Lucy Monroe

Angele refuses to become Crown Prince Zahir's unloved wife out of duty; she will let him go free…but on one condition. The proud Sheikh must give her the wedding night she has dreamed of!

MR AND MISCHIEF
by Kate Hewitt

Sardonic Jason Kingsley is used to women falling at his feet, but relationships are not for him. So why does he find Emily Wood, with her misguided belief in the power of love, irresistibly attractive?

THE BROODING STRANGER
by Maggie Cox

Seeking refuge from her past, Karen Ford comes to Ireland with no intention of getting involved with any man. *Especially* not the brooding stranger she meets one fateful day, who makes a shockingly intimate proposition…

THE GIRL HE NEVER NOTICED
by Lindsay Armstrong

Tycoon Cam Hillier requires a date for this season's fundraising party, and turns to his PA, Liz Montrose, in desperation! Cam's never noticed Liz before…but with no sensible suits or glasses for her to hide behind, that's about to change!

On sale from 3rd June 2011
Don't miss out!

Available at WHSmith, Tesco, ASDA, Eason and all good bookshops

www.millsandboon.co.uk

2 FREE BOOKS
AND A SURPRISE GIFT

We would like to take this opportunity to thank you for reading this
Mills & Boon® book by offering you the chance to take TWO more
specially selected books from the Modern™ series absolutely FREE!
We're also making this offer to introduce you to the benefits of the
Mills & Boon® Book Club™—

- **FREE home delivery**
- **FREE gifts and competitions**
- **FREE monthly Newsletter**
- **Exclusive Mills & Boon Book Club offers**
- **Books available before they're in the shops**

Accepting these FREE books and gift places you under no obligation to buy, you may cancel at any time, even after receiving your free
books. Simply complete your details below and return the entire page
to the address below. You don't even need a stamp!

YES Please send me 2 free Modern books and a surprise gift. I
understand that unless you hear from me, I will receive 4 superb new
books every month for just £3.30 each, postage and packing free. I
am under no obligation to purchase any books and may cancel my
subscription at any time. The free books and gift will be mine to keep
in any case.

Ms/Mrs/Miss/Mr _____ Initials _____

Surname _____

Address _____

_____ Postcode _____

E-mail _____

Send this whole page to: Mills & Boon Book Club, Free Book Offer,
FREEPOST NAT 10298, Richmond, TW9 1BR